et al.

Short Stories

by

Jim Daughton

et al. Short Stories by Jim Daughton

Edited by Susan Stradiotto

Book cover and interior design by Susan Stradiotto.

Printed in the United States of America

First Printing, 2018

Print ISBN-13: 978-1-949357-04-2

www.jimdaughtonbooks.com

Preface

ET AL. (AND OTHERS) stories in this book are like selected short subjects in the old days of movies. After publishing four books (main features), I started writing short stories for my own amusement, and nineteen of them comprise this book. Section A is miscellaneous fiction, Section B is about growing up and growing old, and Section C concerns fishing companions.

I don't know where the ideas for the stories in Section A came from. They concern a variety of subjects, and none of them would be recognized as part of my personal life story. They were fun to write. *A Night at the Westerville Lodge* was written from the point of view of a stuffed animal, *Message from the Cloud* was told by a deceased pet dog, and *Her Majesty's Birthday Note* was written in the style of Sir Arthur Conan Doyle. I hope you have as much fun reading them as I had writing them.

Six of the stories in Section B relate in some way to events of my life. The seventh is about the ultimate futility of preserving memories of a person through photographs, voice recordings, and more technically advanced techniques.

Fishing with a person provides excellent opportunities to know them. Stories in Section C tell of fishing with my son, and then with my son and his friend. *His Last Fly-In* is about an unusual man who was my boss for fifteen years at Honeywell and a friend for much longer than that. *Paxton* concerns a Native American fishing companion living on the Lower Brule reservation in South Dakota.

I am grateful for the help and encouragement from the members of the Western Suburbs Writers Group and the Trillium Woods Writers Group. Also, to Susan Stradiotto for a fine job of editing.

Table of Contents

Section A:

Fiction

Faith Sign

I T WAS THE CRUELEST thing they could have done to poor Ben, taking him off death row and throwing him into solitary with no radio or newspaper to keep tabs on his beloved Chicago Cubs.

Donnie and Jake were bringing Ben to his cell when Donnie said, "The Rangers don't know whether to play baseball with the Cubs or fuck 'em." That was when Ben, in shackles, went crazy and managed to hurt both guards while the other prisoners cheered. To avoid more flare-ups, they put him in solitary confinement, less than three weeks before his execution.

"Ben, do you have faith?" I had asked him when I was first assigned to interview him on death row.

"Nope, Chaplain, don't have much faith left. What's it to ya?"

"Ben, Faith may help you face the ordeal you are going through."

et al.

"Faith hasn't got my sentence commuted. 'Bout the only faith I have left is faith in the Chicago Cubs. You follow them?"

"Sure, aren't they going to the World Series for the first time in 110 years?"

"Right on, Chaplain. I have faith they are going to beat the Rangers. What do you think?"

Awkwardly, I offered, "Faith is like a mustard seed. It starts out small and grows and grows."

Ben's eyebrows lifted a little. I could tell my mustard seed comment had missed its mark. With a skeptical grin, he asked, "If my faith in the Cubs is strong enough, could it help them beat the Rangers?"

"No promises," I said, "but it couldn't hurt. Let's talk."

So that was my introduction to Ben Robinson, on death row for killing an unarmed man in a drug deal gone wrong. "Sure I shot the bastard. He had a nine and was drawing down on me. Had no choice. The fucking police found his gun and hid it. It was a way of gettin' rid of two niggers instead of just one.

Most inmates claim they are innocent, but for some reason, I believed Ben. Maybe it was because he always looked me straight in the eye. Maybe it was because he always told me the truth about smaller things.

He was raised twenty blocks from Wrigley Field—no father, druggie mother, school dropout, and street punk. His passion was the Chicago Cubs. Every year the club let him down just as they had let down three generations of Cub fans before him. But this year was different. As National League champs, they were facing the American League champs in the best-of-seven World Series.

On October tenth, the series was to open in Chicago, but on October eighth, Ben was sent to solitary. No outside communication was allowed, but I persuaded the warden to allow counseling sessions with breakfast every morning. He was sentenced to die by lethal injection October twentieth, the morning after the scheduled seventh game. I promised to bring him full details of the series.

"Good news, Ben," I said as enthusiastically as the morning after game one. "The Cubs won four-zip. Boy, that Green pitched a great game. He allowed only four hits in nine innings. The Cubs are off to a great start."

"I knew that kid had stuff," said Ben. He pressed me for game details, and I told him all I could remember.

"Well, Chaplain maybe this faith stuff has something going for it. Do you think the Cubs will win the series?"

"Don't know if they will or not, Ben. Let's just see how it goes."

et al.

The Cubs lost the next game at home seven-two. The Rangers had been favored from the start and had a great hitting line-up. There were murmurs of "Chicago Jinx" in the newspapers and on television.

The third game was a blowout for Texas, ten-one, and the murmurs became a loud chorus. Ben was disappointed, but insisted I tell him every detail. He still hoped his faith would yet see the Cubs to victory.

Turnip Green pitched the fourth game on three days' rest and again had the Rangers off-stride. The weak-hitting Cubs scored only two runs, but that was enough for a two-one victory for the Cubs. That tied the series two all, but Ben's joy was dampened by the approach of October 20 when he was scheduled to die.

The Cubs won the fifth game six five in ten innings. The Cubs used all of their pitching staff and played their hearts out. Their shortstop, Starlin Castro, fielded brilliantly and drove in four of their six runs with two home runs. Ben smiled weakly after hearing the news, his thoughts seemed elsewhere, probably on his approaching appointment in the death chamber.

What could I say to him or any of them, at least some of whom were innocent of the crime they were convicted of? My calling was to help the afflicted, but maybe I wasn't cut out for this job. "Ben, you will be judged fairly in God's eyes. Does that give you any comfort?"

"You're a good egg, Chaplin, and I don't want to let you down. My life is one big failure. I'm scared shitless about my judgment day. I'm waiting and hoping for a sign that my faith makes a difference." Ben sat slumped back on his cot as I left his cell.

The sixth game was back in Chicago, and the Cubs and their depleted pitching staff were no match for the Ranger hitters. Texas scored six runs in the first inning. The final score was eleven to one. As I left his cell the next morning, Ben was curled up on his cot.

The seventh and final game was scheduled for the evening of the 19th. The winners would be world champions. Ben hoped desperately for a Chicago win, and he would know on that morning.

Then it rained in Chicago. It came down in buckets and persisted. There was no way to hold the game in Wrigley Field, and so the game was delayed by one day.

What a horrible night I spent! I tossed and turned, broke into night sweats. What could I tell Ben in the morning? After such a build-up, how cruel would it be if he went to his death, not knowing?

Struggling with conscience, I decided to invent the game for Ben that he would appreciate the most. What kind of game would it take to restore his faith? I pondered and agonized through a sleepless night.

et al.

When the guard brought Ben's breakfast to his cell the next morning, I entered and sat beside him, prepared with my fabrication.

The guard left, and Ben looked imploringly at me while he nibbled at a piece of toast. Anxiously he asked, "Well, how did it turn out?"

"You aren't going to believe the way the Cubs played. They won one zip. Green pitched great for eight innings but got into trouble in the ninth. The Rangers loaded the bases with two men out, but Green struck out Thurman.

"And how did the Cubs get the run?"

"The Ranger pitcher had a no-hitter going into the bottom half of the inning. The first two batters struck out. Starlin Castro took his first pitch for a strike. The next pitch he hit over Waveland Avenue to win the game for the Chicago Cubs. They're world champions, Ben.'

Two guards and some Texas officials came for Ben. Nobody talked. When we reached the death chamber, they laid Ben on a gurney and strapped him down tight. One of the guards leaned over toward Ben's right ear and said, "The Rangers will make mincemeat out of those pussy Cubs."

My heart stopped. Was this going to be a disaster?

Ben smiled at the guard and said, "You sorry sack-of-shit, the Cubs won one zip with Turnip Green pitching a shutout and Starlin Castro hitting a walk-off home run."

The guard turned away and muttered, "Crazy motherfucker."

Ben was injected with sodium pentothal and went to sleep. Then he snored. After twenty-five minutes a physician from the state pronounced him dead. Witnesses observed Ben's unusually content expression. By mid-afternoon, his body, minus some donated parts, was buried in the prison cemetery. I attended with two Texas officials.

Would God forgive me for trying to give Ben comfort? Tormented and exhausted, I fell into bed early and slept restlessly.

The next morning, I picked up the newspaper and turned to the sports section. The big headline read "Cubs World Champions 1-0." The bylines read "Castro hits walk-off home run" and "Green pitches one-hitter, strikes-out Thurman with bases loaded in ninth." My knees wobbled, and my heart almost exploded in my chest.

A reporter for the Associated Press witnessing the execution had heard what Ben had told the guard. The reporter even had Ben's words in black and white in his official execution notebook. The guard later confirmed the quote.

et al.

The story made Ben a prison legend. Most of the public believed the happenings were just unusual coincidences. As for me, I no longer doubt my calling to minister to the condemned.

Creed of the Range

*J*IM WRIGHT ENTERED GERSHEL'S General Store in Winnett, Montana and walked to the back counter, his cowboy boots clumping out a slow rhythm on the wood floor. He didn't bother to put his Stetson under his arm.

"Hi Jim," said the clerk. "A little chill in the air, huh?"

"Yep, Sally. Seems like it always gets cool in mid-November."

"What can I do for ya' today?" she asked.

"I need to buy a deer license."

"Bout time," Sally said. "Season opens Saturday. Dig out your driver's license and a twenty-dollar bill and I'll get ya fixed up pronto."

While waiting for his license, Jim wandered through the store perusing guns, ammunition, duck calls, and paper targets. Then he ran into Justin Hardin, who had grown up in Petroleum County about ten miles south of Winnett. Either he or Jim could have doubled as the prototype cowboy. They had creased, tanned faces and wore long-sleeved flannel shirts and blue jeans held up by leather belts sporting over-sized large brass buckles. "Hi Justin. What brings you back here from the Fish and Wildlife Protection Headquarters?"

"Good to see you, Jim. Oh, even FWP has a heart. They are letting me do a wildlife survey back in my old stomping grounds. I still have some family here, ya know."

"Your brother speaking with you again?"

"Not yet, but he'll get over it. He shoulda known I couldn't let him have more than a possession limit of pheasants. I swore to uphold the game laws of Montana."

"He says he was just one bird over, and it was just a counting mistake."

"The law is the law. I couldn't treat him different just because he's my brother. He'll come around. Let's talk of more pleasant things. How's Marge?"

"Oh, she's pretty good. Maybe a little lonesome since Polly went off to college. They write each other weekly and talk on the phone every day. But now it's just Marge and me on ten sections of prairie, pretty much twenty-four hours a day, every day."

"This can be a lonely country," said Justin. "I hear the county is down to fewer than five hundred people, and almost two hundred of them live right here in Winnett."

Sally called to Jim, "Got your license ready, Jim. It's on the counter."

"Good luck hunting this weekend, Jim," said Justin.

"We need it," said Jim. "Our freezer's plumb empty. The only meat we've had for the past few days is canned tuna or a stewed hen when Sally sacrifices one out of our chicken house."

Jim put his license in his shirt pocket and walked to the pickup truck where his wife was already sitting in the passenger's seat, and with the week's groceries and salt and minerals for the cattle in the bed. "Did you buy your license yet, Marge?"

"Yep. Got it when I went to the feed store."

"And did you mail Polly her monthly check?"

"Sure did. Wish we could send her more that $100. That doesn't go far."

"Justin Hardin was in the sporting goods store."

"He's a nice man. Too bad about his wife," said Marge.

"Yeah. He's lonely. He's throwing all his energy into his work."

They drove in silence for twelve miles along a blacktopped county road and then turned onto an unpaved road with a telephone and electric lines running alongside the mile road to their house. Two tall wooden poles with a chain strung between welcomed them into their parking area. Attached to the middle of the chain was a length of rebar steel bent into a 'J' and almost completely surrounded by a circle. Set back from the road a hundred feet stood the small, two-story, clapboard-siding house where Jim was born, a house that Jim's father (also a Jim) had built.

He unloaded the cattle's salt and then helped unload the week's provisions from the pickup and carried them into the kitchen. "What's for supper Sweet Marge?"

"Mac and cheese, head lettuce salad, and I think I've still got time yet this afternoon to bake an applesauce cake.

"Sounds good. But wouldn't it be great to have some meat for a change?"

"If you weren't so stubborn, we could butcher one of our cattle and have beef whenever we want."

"Marge, we need all the income from the cattle we can get. We just can't afford to sacrifice one. We're just making ends meet as it is. With my buck and doe and your buck and doe, we should have all the meat we need for a year. Right now I've got to go look after the cows on the back section. I should be back before dark."

He walked out past the hen house to the three-walled machine shed that was open to the south. A hay baler and his red Farmall were inside. He filled the tractor with gas from a 500-gallon tank and drove cross-country to where his herd of ninety

Hereford cows had gathered waiting to be hayed. He did a fast count to make sure they were all there. He knew each one by her face. Their calves had all been trucked to feeder operations two weeks before, and the poor mothers were almost over their losses. If the bulls, Shorty and Max, had done their job, a new crop of calves would come next March and April.

A fence surrounded two long rows of giant round hay bales. Jim undid a gate, and using the forklift on his tractor, hauled four bales onto the pasture. He cut the plastic and twine from the bales and rolled out the hay. It was good quality hay with a fair amount of alfalfa mixed in with the coarse grasses. The cows celebrated by munching their newly found bounty.

He then started a gas engine powering a deep-well pump, and he filled two large stock tanks with water. Some of the cows wandered over from the hay bales and took big drinks. The cattle had all they needed for the time being. Later in the year as the snow and cold weather came, Jim would move the cattle near a large shed that would offer at least some shelter for the creatures.

As he drove back towards the house, he saw a deer on a ridge. He took his 30.06 off the rack in back of his head and peered through its scope. It was a buck mule deer, a big one. This was Thursday. His license wouldn't be valid until Saturday morning, but the freezer was empty, and he was very unlikely to see a bigger buck in the season. Who was to know? The deer was out about 150 yards, but the bullet wouldn't drop more than an inch at that distance. He took careful aim and pulled the trigger.

et al.

The deer jumped, ran twenty feet, and crumpled. Jim drove over and cut its throat with a knife. He waited about a half hour for it to bleed out, and then field-dressed the deer, leaving the entrails for the coyotes. After a struggle, he managed to load the carcass on the forklift, drove home and into the machine shed. Using a block and tackle he hung the buck from a rafter. He took a buck tag from his shirt pocket, carefully dated it for Saturday, and secured it to the right antler of the big buck. He walked to his house.

"Where have you been?" asked Marge. "It's dark."

"Shot a deer. Might dress out over 200 pounds."

"Good Lord. The season isn't open."

"Not to worry, my little stage hen. It's hanging in the back of the machine shed. No one will see it there. I'll cut it up on Saturday."

They consumed their vegetarian meal in silence. As they ate applesauce cake and drank coffee, Marge had an idea. "Would there be any harm in taking the back straps off the deer so we can have them tomorrow for lunch?"

"Why Darling, that sounds like a wonderful idea. I'll get 'em while you do the dishes."

Jim went to the machine shed carrying his sharpest knife. He peeled the deer's hide away from both sides of its backbone and removed two long, slender pieces of meat about 12 inches long, one and a half inches in diameter in the middle, and tapering to a point at one end. He carried them in a stainless-steel pan back to the house. "Here ya go, my pet. Just like you ordered."

"Boy, they look wonderful. I can hardly wait for tomorrow's lunch."

The next morning, Jim looked after the cattle, and Marge made rolls. She baked and made bread almost every day. She had bought bacon in town, and she fried about half a pound so it was transparent and very flexible. About an hour before lunch, she cut the backstraps into one-inch-thick pieces and wrapped each piece with bacon, sticking a toothpick through the bacon and meat to hold it together. She set the table with buttered rolls, hot baked beans, and chopped head lettuce with Italian dressing. Then she heated her large cast iron pan and started frying the meat.

Jim was walking toward the house when a light green pickup with FWP overlaid with an image of the state of Montana on the door drove into the yard. Out stepped Justin Hardin. "Hi Jim," he said.

"Hi Justin. Good to see ya. You're just in time for lunch. Can ya' come in?"

"Don't mind if I do. But first I got to report my whereabouts to the folks in Glasgow. Government work, ya know."

et al.

Jim went into the kitchen. "Marge, you have to set another place for lunch. Justin drove in."

"Oh God, Jim. Why did you invite him? We could get into big trouble. I can't cook anything for lunch at this hour but this venison. What are we going to do?"

"We don't have a choice about inviting him. You grew up in Montana. You know as well as I do that anyone showing up at dinnertime must be invited. If we get into trouble, well, that's life."

Justin entered the house and hung his hat on one of the pegs on the back porch. He washed his hands in the little bathroom off the kitchen and sat down at the table.

Marge was just finishing the backstraps, taking care that the bacon got a little crisp but leaving the venison rare. They ate family style passing around a platter of meat and bowls of salad and beans and helping themselves to freshly baked rolls. Marge seemed a little nervous, but she popped up to replenish food in serving dishes when they were empty. They ate all of everything and then drank coffee and ate applesauce cake leftover from the previous evening.

"My, what a meal," Justin said. "And those veal tenderloins were just like my Mary used to make."

"Glad you liked them," said Marge.

"Well, got to be going. Thanks so much for the meal," said Justin.

"Don't mention it," said Jim.

Jim and Marge walked out into the yard and waved goodbye as Justin drove off. "Jim, do ya think he didn't know that was venison?"

"Honey, off course he knew. He's been eating deer meat since he was weaned. And that comment about veal. He knows there ain't no rancher in this part of Montana that eats veal."

"Justin is such a straight shooter," said Marge. "Why didn't he come after us?"

"Our invitation to dinner obeyed a commandment of the range more important than the fish and game rules of Montana, and Justin couldn't enforce a lesser law because we obeyed a greater one," said Jim.

Message from the Cloud

I'M SENDING THIS MESSAGE and hoping for a miracle, hoping that Mistress will get it. In the spirit world, things are confused. There are so many of us milling around that communications with the right party are really difficult, particularly with the material world, which we're not really supposed to enter. Competition from all that computer stuff in the cloud doesn't make things any easier. This attempt is like placing a message in a bottle and casting it into the sea, hoping it will be opened some day by the right party.

My name is Sable. Anyway, that is what Mistress called me. In life I was a four-pound toy poodle with light brown, curly hair. My mother was Laura's Pride and my father Ludwig Alfonzo, although I never saw much of him, and I had a brother, Peanut Butter. I was put up for adoption when I was six weeks old, and a nice lady took me home and fed me and petted me. But a mean man living with her didn't like me. Once I was on the bed and he knocked me off and kicked me across the room, breaking two of my ribs. The nice lady decided to find me a new home. She asked another nice lady she knew if she would take me. "Only for a weekend to see how things work out," she said. That was how I met Mistress.

Mistress lived in what they call a town home. The first weekend there she introduced me to potty training. "Potty on the paper. Potty on the paper," she would say, and set me on newspapers spread out on the floor. Soon I got the idea. I could sniff out the newspapers and learned to poop and pee on them. That must have pleased Mistress because she petted me and squeezed me and said nice things to me. And she gave me my name. I knew she would keep me. We really were buddies.

Mistress had to work most weekdays, so she left me in the morning and came home in the late afternoon. Boy, was I lonesome. I was really sad when she left, but really happy when she came home. At night I slept with her, lying in the crook of her arm. When I wanted to go under the covers, I would scratch her politely. When I got out of bed, I would grab some item of clothing from her closet, and carry it in my teeth past her with my head straight, but my eyes looking sideways to see if she was paying attention. Mistress thought that very funny. Things were great with just the two of us.

Then Alpha started showing up. I was a little jealous because Mistress paid so much attention to him. I wasn't sure I liked him. One day he lay down on the floor by me so we were eye-to-eye. Then he made woof-woof noises. Without knowing why, I made woof-woof noises back. Alpha had taught me to bark. After that, we were buddies, too.

Mistress took me to see the doctor for shots and a small operation. This operation meant that I could never have puppies. I was pretty sick afterwards, and Mistress felt so bad for me. I tried to cheer her up.

Then Mistress and Alpha decided to mate. Mistress and I moved to Alpha's house, and then my life changed. There were two others in that house, Boy and Cat. I didn't like Boy, and I barked at him, particularly if he came close to our bedroom where Mistress, Alpha, and I slept. Once Boy came home after school before Mistress and Alpha came home from work, and naturally, I barked at him. Well, he took a water pistol and got me wet. I got even by laying a little deposit by his bedroom door, which was counter to my potty training. Boy was mad, but Mistress understood. Boy and I never did get along.

Cat was another story. Of course, we were natural enemies. So I would bark and snap at her, and she would hiss and try to scratch me. But do you know what? She was company during the day. I would chase her around the hallway, through to living room, back through the kitchen and to the hallway again. When we tried to make a turn on the linoleum in the kitchen, our paws lost traction and we both would slide and spin. Sometimes Cat would bury under a rug on her back, and when I moved in to bite her, she would bat my head ten times in a second with her front paws, that were, thank God, declawed. If I did deliver a little bite, my mouth would get fur in it. If Mistress was home, she helped me get the fur out of my mouth.

At night, Boy went to his bedroom, and Mistress and Alpha went to our bed. Usually, I slept under the covers with Mistress, but sometimes I slept on Alpha's stomach. Cat wanted to sleep with the three of us, too. You could imagine what I thought of that. The second she would hop up on the bed, I would growl and chase her off. She was persistent, though, and often in the morning when I got up, I found her sleeping by Alpha's feet at the foot of the bed. Eventually Cat was allowed to sleep there, but she couldn't come any closer to the head of the bed without feeling my ire.

I have to tell you about Auntie May. When Mistress and Alpha went away for a few days, I got to go to Auntie May's house. Although I missed my family, staying with Auntie May was a treat. She was so nice to me, and she took care of so many other dogs that I was never lonely. But I was very happy when Mistress came back for me.

Mistress quit working, and then we had more time together. Often we would go out for coffee in the morning. I would sit by her in the front seat and off we would go. When Mistress went into the store, I would stand on my hind legs and look out the driver's seat window. I could hear people say how cute I was. These happy days lasted until we moved to a brand new house.

Cat couldn't adjust to the new place. She had been born in the old house and had scarcely set a paw outside it in her whole life. The first night we were in the new house, Cat perched on a high shelf in the laundry room, yowling. Mistress felt sorry for Cat and slept on the floor so Cat could sleep with her. Mistress was afraid Cat's barf would ruin her new house, so she sent her to live with Boy. I was missing my best playmate, and I heard that Cat missed me, too.

Then Mistress got very sick for a period. I was able to give her some comfort and eventually she pulled through, and we had a few more good years. Alpha was part of the pack now, and when he traveled, I waited at the head of the stair at night for him to come home.

And then I started to get sick. I got very skinny and cranky. I bit both Mistress and Alpha. My potty training forgotten, I had to stay in a room with papers lying on the floors and even taped along the walls. I was in pain all the time. Sometimes I would get my head in a corner and couldn't figure a way out. One time when Alpha was gone on a trip, Mistress took me to the doctor and I heard him say, "It's time."

The doctor gave me a shot, and it hurt a little, so I gave a little yelp. But then the pain was gone, and I felt free. I was aware of Mistress weeping as I entered the spirit world, but didn't know how to comfort her, to tell her it was all right. A few times since I have managed to get into her dream world to let her know I was free. I run to her and lick her face, and she pets my ears and tells

25

me how good I smell. She wakes up a little happier, but I know she still mourns for me. And I know she feels guilty for sending me to the spirit world.

So here is the purpose of this message. If by chance Mistress should receive it, or if you bump into her, I really want her to know I loved every minute we spent together, and I want to thank her for freeing me from pain and torment that day at the doctor's office. I know it was very hard for her to do, and I really appreciated it.

I ran into Cat the other day in the spirit world, but it wasn't the same without Mistress and Alpha. We know that someday the other two will be joining us, and then we will be at peace, just the four of us, just as we were with me in the crook of Mistress's arm and Cat by Alpha's feet, in our happiest times together.

Larceny at Sea

Part One

THE CRUISE SHIP SEAFARER had left Shanghai the night of March first and now plied the Straight of Formosa toward Hong Kong where she was to dock the following morning. The South China Sea's choppy waters made for tricky walking on deck for passengers. The waves jerked the ship in quick, unexpected directions, and passengers walked with feet spread and hands near a rail. But Rolf Derek walked briskly and confidently while inspecting the ship. He had been the Master of the *Seafarer* for the past eight years. He was six foot four, blonde, very fit, and his ready smile and flashing blue eyes endeared him to every female passenger.

Captain Derek entered the office of the hotel director, Sven Larson. He was tall like the captain, but darker and slender as a reed. Sven rarely smiled. A cruise ship is, after all, a floating hotel, a business. It is imperative that the hotel manager and the captain work as a team. Both wore their blue uniforms. "A very

et al.

good morning, Sven," said Rolf in a deep baritone with a Norwegian accent.

"What are the seas going to be like, Captain?"

"Looks like we are going to get some larger swells between here and Hong Kong, but less choppy conditions. You should continue to warn passengers to be careful while standing or walking."

"Will do, Captain. Sounds like more cases of sea sicknesses and fewer broken bones."

"The cruise line advertises adventure and excitement for the passengers but would vastly prefer nothing unusual happens. Just board the cruisers, sail them around, and deboard them. No fuss. Unplanned events reflect poorly on the captain."

"Unfortunately, you speak the truth."

"What's the count, Sven?"

"We've got two hundred eighty-five world-cruisers and two hundred ninety segmenters, Captain. We netted an additional twenty-one segmenters on our stop in Shanghai. We're pretty near capacity."

"Any passengers I should pay special attention to?"

"One couple made the *Wall Street Journal* a few months back. John Vogel and Sylvia Porter Vogel cofounded PartyLine, the social media company that was bought a year ago by

DoubleTalk. John provided technical smarts and she the financial savvy. It's a formal night tonight and I have them at your table. You already know the other two couples, the Goodes and the Doles, both couples are seasoned world-cruisers."

"How long will the Vogels be with us?"

"Just this segment. They get off in Singapore."

PRECEDING DINNER, THE CAPTAIN introduced himself and the crew to passengers in the Constellation Theater. Afterwards, passengers scattered to one of the ship's four restaurants. The Captain's Table was set for eight in the Compass Rose, the formal dining room. Helen Schneider, the security officer, accompanied Rolf, both in formal white uniforms with gold stripes. She was a blonde, blue-eyed thirty-something German and had been at one time a highly ranked amateur skier. The Goodes and Doles were in conventional evening dress, tuxedos for the men and gowns for the women with the women wearing their best matching jewelry.

The Vogels kicked off the introductions. "I am Sylvia Vogel and this is my husband, John. We are very pleased to meet you."

People politely introduced themselves around the table. The captain and Helen were relaxed in this setting, but the others sat erect with eyes darting around the dining room. After Father Collins said a short blessing followed by a round of champagne

et al.

toasts, the atmosphere loosened. Four tuxedoed waiters stood by their assigned couples at the Captain's Table, took orders, and then disappeared to the kitchen.

"I understand you two started a media company," said the captain.

"We did," said John. Although neatly dressed, his brown hair was unruly and the lenses in his eyeglasses were unusually thick and wanted cleaning. "It took us five years to get PartyLine going. We had help though, major help. Sam Lieu, as much as I, was the genius behind our concept. Sylvia and I plan to meet with him in Hong Kong. We hope we get to work together again. We thought we had it made after the sale to DoubleTalk, but that company took bankruptcy at the end of last year."

Waiters appeared again with hors d'oeuvres: crab and shrimp cocktails, escargot, and tuna tartar. Following that course, the waiters delivered soups to their assigned couples.

"We are trying to raise venture capital for a brand new company," announced John. "It's hard, though, because investors are scared off by the failure of DoubleTalk."

"If at first you don't succeed...," said Sylvia. She was a slender, buxom redhead in a red dress. She was left-handed, and as she spread a big pat of butter on a piece of French bread, a very large diamond in her wedding ring sparkled in the multiplicity of lights from the dining room chandeliers. Sylvia's words were slightly slurred from pre dinner drinks and champagne.

"How did you two meet?" asked Nicky Goode.

"We met at Stanford," said Sylvia. "John was in computer science and I was in business. Together with Sam Lieu we cooked up the idea for PartyLine while in grad school."

"Sylvia handled all the business end," said John. "I have absolutely no head for money."

"Well, you are fortunate to have gone to Stanford," said Mr. Dole. "Not everyone can get in there."

"We were unbelievably lucky," said John. "Both Sylvia and I are from poor families. Sylvia is from Arkansas and I came from Brooklyn. We were so fortunate to win support from our teachers and professors and to get scholarships. Otherwise we wouldn't be here."

"Yeah," said Sylvia. probably have three kids and a farmer husband. I like this a lot better." John gazed at her and smiled.

As always at the Captain's Table, the food and service were exceptional. Waiters brought salads, main courses, and desserts in turn, and to finish the meal, coffee and tea. Everyone at the Captain's Table then rose and headed to a puppet show in the Constellation Theater except for Sylvia, who made her way to the casino, and John, who returned to his cabin to write software code for their proposed company.

et al.

THE NEXT MORNING, SEAFARER was on the open sea. Helen arose before the captain. "Wasn't that some kind of ring, Rolf?"

The captain rubbed the sleepiness from his eyes. "I'll say. How big a diamond was that? Fifteen or twenty carats. Larger? There have been a lot of rich women on this ship with fancy jewelry, but I never saw anything that large before."

"It was just huge." Helen, already dressed in whites, paused as she approached the door and slowly opened it. The aisle was clear, and she whispered, "Bye, Rolf," and was out the door.

Captain Derek thought, *too bad we have to sneak around like this. The crew knows about us, of course. There are no secrets from the stewardesses. Helen and I are both married, but what can you do about loneliness when you are away from home six months at a time? I wouldn't want my Margaret to know, but she would understand. Wouldn't she? And it's not like Helen is a passenger or crew. That could get me fired.*

This day most women busied themselves with getting their hair done and planning their dress for the formal night that evening. The cocktail hour was something of a jewelry show. Large rubies, sapphires, and emeralds decorated rings, necklaces, and bracelets that sparkled in the ship's lighting. And of course, there were the diamonds, and Sylvia's ring was a big hit. With some nervous hesitation, a few passengers asked to look at it up close, and Sylvia granted them an audience. One slightly tipsy jewelry magnate held Sylvia's hand and squinted through the stone at the point of a pencil held close to the ring. "That proves it's real," he joked. "Diamonds bend light too much to see straight through them." Sylvia gave him a disapproving look and turned away.

THE SHIP DOCKED AS planned at 0800 on March third in Hong Kong.

Passengers flocked ashore to one of the best shopping ports in the world. Clothing of all kinds, jewelry, perfumes, and watches. Even prescription glasses in an hour. Product quality varied from the finest to shoddy knockoffs. Harbor ferries rushed at high speeds to various sites in Hong Kong. Passengers reboarded the ship laden with shopping bags of loot.

Just before the ship departed from Hong Kong on the evening of the fourth of March, Sven called the Vogel's penthouse cabin. "John, would you mind coming to my office? I have something to discuss with you."

"Be there in five minutes."

John entered Sven's office. "Please have a seat."

John sat across the desk from Sven. "What do you have for me?"

"You gave us a credit card to use for ship's charges, and American Express rejected the billing for your wife's gambling losses the other night. The bill was about $2200. I suppose there is some mistake or oversight somewhere, but for us that is a substantial amount. Would you please correct this problem?"

"I'm terribly embarrassed, Sven," said John, his face turning red. "We have an international cell phone, and I'll call my bank right away and deposit the funds to cover the bill on the credit card, and several thousand dollars extra. I will tell Sylvia not to charge anything more on our ship's account."

"Thank you, John. I knew it would be easily corrected."

The next day the *Seafarer* sailed on the South China Sea bound for Viet Nam. Rolf and Sven drank their morning coffees in the Topsider Café.

"How are our entrepreneurial guests doing, Sven?"

"Oh, there was a little glitch. The credit card company bounced his wife's casino bill. But Mr. Vogel took care of it," said Sven.

"That doesn't look too good for the financial genius she is supposed to be."

"I got a little suspicious about their finances and dug into the details of their deal with DoubleTalk. They got twenty-five million dollars in cash and two hundred million dollars in DoubleTalk stock. The stock became worthless just before their restriction to sell expired. Maybe they overextended their finances before they realized the stock would become worthless."

"Well, like she said the other night at dinner, 'Try, try again.' Only it's sounding like they may have trouble getting started again," said the captain.

"Excuse me, Sven, I saw your office door was open, and I hope you don't mind my barging in like this." Sylvia Vogel was wearing shorts and a halter top. A wave of lavender perfume accompanied her into the office.

"Not at all, Mrs. Vogel. Please have a seat."

"I understand you don't want me to use your casino. This is a day at sea and the casino will be open tonight. I really love to gamble. Just this one evening, I would like to give it a shot." She bent over his desk displaying her ample bosom.

Sven was perplexed. Had her husband told her that the ship had forbid her to go to the casino? For an instant he hesitated. "I guess, if your husband doesn't care, I won't object."

"Oh, he doesn't care what I do. I can do anything. By the way, drop by the casino at closing time, and maybe we can get to know each other better."

She wiggled and jiggled out of Sven's office leaving him a little short of breath. Sven had no intention of getting involved with a passenger, especially a married one. His wife might, probably would, forgive him, but the cruise line wouldn't. That could spell the end to a twenty-year career at sea. But still as she

et al.

had walked away, his nether brain wondered if she were a natural redhead.

Part Two

ON THE SIXTH OF March, *Seafarer* docked for a day at Nha Trang, Viet Nam. It was an opportunity for the passengers to see some of rural Viet Nam where they raised rice exactly the same way as they did one thousand years ago. Oxen plowed through flooded paddies, and women selected individual rice plants from bundles on their backs and planted them in the mud. At harvest time they still threshed grain by hand. The Vogels blended in with the other tourists on tours and shipboard activities.

The next morning the ship's second stop in Viet Nam was Ho Chi Minh City, which some still called Saigon. They arrived at 0900 and weren't scheduled to shove off until 1600 the next day. Some three decades earlier Saigon had seen the defeat of western powers in a bloody war that left the country devastated, but since then the city has become vital and growing, and surprisingly friendly to westerners. Entire families of four ride on single motorbikes. Pedestrians learned to walk across busy streets at a constant pace without stopping, and vehicles timed their speeds to avoid them. Everything kept moving. Stopping could cause a bad accident. The ship's passengers poured off the ship for tours on both mornings and returned to the ship on both evenings.

The ship resumed the voyage on the Gulf of Thailand near the dinner hour when the captain's phone rang. "My wife's ring has been stolen!" cried John Vogel, his voice trembling. The captain could hear Mrs. Vogel wailing in the background.

"I'll get to your suite right away."

Captain Derek called over the intercom, "Code red, suite ten ten. Code red, suite ten ten." Then he headed to the Vogel's cabin where he knew Sven and Helen would join him. Helen actually beat him there and was holding the sobbing and shaking Sylvia. Sven arrived only a couple of steps behind the captain.

"Alright," said the captain, "Let's try to settle down and understand this situation." He stood erect and projected calm as he would even if the ship were sinking.

Still choking back tears, Sylvia explained. "This afternoon I was going to the pool. I took off my ring and put it in the dressing-table drawer instead of in the safe where I usually put it. I didn't think anything about it until I was getting ready for dinner. I was about to put the ring on, but the ring wasn't there. I've looked everywhere in our cabin and so has John. It's just gone, gone." Sylvia went on another crying jag. John put his arm around her, offering comfort.

"It has been my experience," said the captain, "that often the missing item is found, sometimes in unexpected places. But to allow for the possibility of a theft, we will follow ship's procedures. Helen, prepare a list of all personnel who used their room keycards to enter this suite any time today. You and Sven should question each of them as to what they know...what they saw in the room. Look for suspicious behavior—nervousness, heavy perspiration, no eye contact. Also, please initiate a search for the missing item in this suite and everywhere Mrs. Vogel went this afternoon. By the way, is the ring insured?"

"Yes," said Mr. Vogel. "It's insured for its full value by Transamerica."

"You should call them right away and make them aware of a potential loss," said the captain.

"Oh, what can we do?" cried Sylvia. "Someone took part of my heart when they took the ring."

John Vogel explained, "It was a symbol to us, not just of our love, but of the success of our five-year struggle in making PartyLine a success. I bought it one week after we got the cash from the sale to Doubletalk."

"If this involves a lot of money, a Transamerica representative will probably want to join the ship and investigate personally, "said the captain.

"We paid twenty-three million dollars for it," said Sylvia. "It's from the Jewel Steinhart estate."

"We will be in Thailand tomorrow for two days, but that probably won't be enough time for the insurance people to arrive," said Sven. "We will arrive in Singapore on the thirteenth and will be there for two days. If the ring doesn't turn up, I would suppose Transamerica would want to come aboard. I would suggest that port might be a good place for the insurance people to meet the ship if they want to visit the scene."

"I'll complete the crew interrogations and provide a full report in the morning," said Helen. "I will round up a search group and go over this cabin with a fine-toothed comb this evening. Mr. and Mrs. Vogel, would you please open your suite safe and all baggage, so we can assure that the ring isn't here?"

"Of course," they replied.

"It's my duty as Captain to notify our home office of the potential theft. I will forward Helen's report by 0900 tomorrow morning."

"And I will notify TransAmerica right now," said John Vogel.

AS THE SHIP SAILED the Gulf of Thailand the next morning at 0900, Captain Derek, Sven, and Helen drank coffee in the captain's office with the door closed.

"No trace of the ring, and we looked everywhere," said Helen.

"Just the kind of thing I don't need," said Rolf. "I'm afraid the cruise line will be all over my ass."

et al.

Helen continued, "We checked security records, and the only crew members entering the cabin were two maids, a repairman fixing the hot water in one of the showers, and the butler who brought in afternoon snacks. I will go over the interview records one at a time."

"We interviewed the Filipino stewardesses, Christine Montenz, first. We searched her living quarters. She has worked with us for two years and has a flawless record. Mrs. Montenz was in tears and protesting her family couldn't survive if she lost her job. They wouldn't be able to build a planned house. She couldn't offer any information about the missing ring.

"Monica Felipe also cried and was terrified during the interview. Ms. Felipe has been with us only a year but has a good record. She offered no new information and also gave us permission to search her quarters.

"Umberto Delmonte was called by John to fix their shower that didn't provide enough hot water. He was there from two o'clock until three, during the period before the ring went missing. He didn't seem to know anything new, but he pointed out that people could enter the cabin by walking on a railing from an adjacent veranda, if the Vogel's veranda door was open, which it was. So we also talked to the resident of the adjoining cabin, and performed a search, but found nothing."

"Samu Gandhi delivered afternoon snacks to the cabin during the critical time period. He was insulted that he was being questioned and had nothing to add. He also permitted a search of his living area.

"All quarters were searched without discovering anything, and I submitted the report as you requested," concluded Helen. "We came up empty."

"I guess this should now a matter between the Vogels and TransAmerica," said Captain Derek. "But I'm afraid this could go hard on us."

"You are correct, Rolf." Sven looked tired and worried. "We, the company, will probably be sued by both the Vogels and TransAmerica for lax security. When a lot of money is at stake, lawyers come out of the woodwork."

"What else could we do short of strip searching everyone getting on and off the ship?" said Helen. "You obviously couldn't run a cruise that way."

"Thank God things like this don't happen very often," said the Captain. His shoulders slumped, and he sighed. *This won't look good on my record.*

SEAFARER DOCKED IN THAI ports the tenth and eleventh of March. Passengers shopped for silk goods, visited parlors for ten-dollar foot massages, and ate world famous Thai foods. The Vogels slouched and frowned, but they did their best to carry on normal activities, touring Bangkok and eating dinner in the

et al.

Compass Rose. Silvia's bare left ring finger prompted whispers all over the ship. The ship then sailed on the Gulf of Thailand on March twelfth. An insurance representative was to visit the ship in Singapore the next day.

The first person to board the ship wore a dark blue business suit, unusual attire for the tropical climate of Singapore. He strode deliberately up the gangplank and was met by Captain Derek who extended his hand and said, "Welcome aboard. Richard Sicher, I presume."

"You presume correctly, Captain." He deposited folded sunglasses carefully in his coat pocket. "I am the special agent representing TransAmerica Insurance Company. First, I would like to meet with the Vogels and then with your security staff. Do you have a meeting room I can use?"

"Of course. You can use my office if you wish. The Vogels are there already. I'll take you."

The Vogels repeated the story of the theft, and Sicher listened carefully for any differences between their story and Helen's report. The insurance agent informed the Vogels, "As you know, we have to be entirely satisfied the ring is missing. Assuming we conclude it is, the company has a right to replace the ring with an equivalent piece instead of the face value of the policy. There is also a one time charge of one-thousand dollars per theft incident. Do you have any questions?"

John said, "The ring is one of a kind. I really doubt you can find an equivalent piece." Sylvia began to weep, and John put his arm around her. "We are scheduled to disembark here in Singapore, and we have a plane to catch. Is this all you need us for?"

"Just sign the insurance claim of loss and have it notarized. That's all we need at this time. Please be patient. Claims this large may take a year to settle." Mr. Sicher went to the door and said, "Thank you Sylvia and John. We will be in touch." As the Vogels exited Sicher requested a meeting with the security staff, consisting of Helen, Sven, and the captain. The captain introduced the others to Mr. Sicher.

"Ms. Schneider, we noted that the ship missed a monthly security exercise last November. Other than that, your security records seemed in order."

"None of us here were on the ship in November," said the captain. "The staff turned over in Fort Lauderdale in December, and that's when we came aboard."

"Have you any reason to suspect the ring isn't missing? We are talking about a great deal of money, and we have to check every angle."

"We certainly saw Mrs. Vogel wearing the ring on the ship, and she was obviously very attached to it," said Helen. "She was distraught when it went missing. We questioned every crew member with access to the Vogel cabin on the day of the crime and

et al.

have searched every square inch of their cabin. It's definitely missing."

"What would the thief do with the ring?" asked Sven. "I would think the culprit would have a hard time getting rid of it."

"There's some truth in that," replied the agent. "But there are two possibilities. The first is the black market for very large diamonds in the Orient. The stone is indeed unique. The D flawless round cut diamond weighing 23.10 carats is the only one just like it in the world. There will probably never be another. We'll get the word out so everyone in the diamond trade will know it was stolen. The Triad, a Chinese-based crime organization out of Hong Kong, makes a market for stolen jewelry, and it might find a buyer for the big stone. Or the diamond could be cut into three or four smaller diamonds. After cutting, the total value would be reduced by about half, but GIA certificates for the smaller stones could be forged, and the chances of getting caught would be negligible."

"I have a hard time believing any of our crew could have taken it," said the captain. "And we interviewed everyone with access to the Vogel's suite very thoroughly. I don't think any of them were lying."

"It is still possible that a crew member took it, but there may be another possibility," said the agent. "Our preliminary investigation has shown that the Vogels are in financial difficulty. They have unpaid debts of more than five million dollars. Their creditors have already contacted us to verify that the Vogels have filed for the loss. If the ring disappears, the insurance settlement might bail the Vogels out of trouble. So, maybe the Vogels hid the ring somewhere."

"Wouldn't it have been simpler to just sell the ring?" asked the captain. "That would give them plenty to settle their debts."

Sicher frowned. "They are having problems raising capital for a new company. Maybe this was a case of selling the ring now and collecting insurance money later."

"Can we help you further?" asked the captain.

"I would like to inspect the cabin where the crime occurred and talk with the crew members who had access to the cabin."

"I'll take you to the suite, and the crew will talk with you. I will arrange it."

The insurance agent's requests were met, and he and the Vogels left the ship and flew back to the United States. The ship sailed outbound for Mumbai, India with stops along the way.

ON THE MORNING OF the twenty-sixth of March, the day before the scheduled docking in Mumbai, Captain Derek went to his office. He noticed something sparkling in the middle of his desk. It was a ring, *the* ring! He called for Helen and Sven to come immediately.

et al.

"Holy shit, what do we do now?" asked the captain. For a time they just stared at the ring.

"Obviously we have to contact our home office, the Vogels, and TransAmerica," said Helen. "What else?"

"I had hoped we could fade into the background on this matter," said Sven.

"You two are witnesses," said Captain Derek. "Note and record the time and place this ring was found."

"Looks like it needs to be cleaned a bit," said Helen. "Want me to take care of that?"

"No. I will put it in the ship's safe just as we found it. Please take care of notifying the appropriate parties, Helen. We stay two days in Mumbai. Maybe the Vogels and Mr. Sicher could meet us there."

Part Three

AS THE SHIP APPROACHED Mumbai, India on the twenty-seventh of March, Helen came to the captain's office. "Mr. Sicher will meet us this morning, but the Vogels won't. Sylvia asked that we send her the ring. She must be having difficulty starting the new business. I thought she would be overjoyed with the news, but if she was happy, I couldn't tell it from her voice. Mr. Vogel said he was back at work with DoubleTalk, or what was left of it, struggling to get the company back in operation."

"Well, at least TransAmerica ought to be happy," said Rolf.

Mr. Sicher came on board with his ever serious look. The captain thought Sicher was wearing the same business suit he wore in Singapore. It was, however, well pressed, and the collar of his white shirt looked starchy stiff. "I have brought with me Michael Stern, who is an expert in precious stones," said the agent introducing Mr. Stern to the captain. Mr. Stern also wore a dark business suit. He was short and portly, and he spoke with a German accent. "Welcome aboard, you two. Please come with me to my office. I will have the ring brought there."

As they were seated in the captain's office, Helen produced a small box and set it on the table. Mr. Sicher opened the box, removed the ring, and handed it to Mr. Stern. Mr. Stern used a jeweler's loupe to examine the diamond from several different directions and emitted a few "ahas," then using pocket tools, he demounted the diamond from its platinum setting. He noted the jeweler's mark inside the setting and made a small drawing of it in a notebook. From a briefcase he drew out a small scale. He weighed the stone and emitted another "aha." Then, with deliberation, he pronounced, "This is not the Steinhart diamond. You probably know the four C's of diamonds: cut, color, clarity, and carats. The Jenifer Sinclair diamond was a round cut, D color, flawless clarity, and weighted 23.01 carats. This diamond is also round cut, has good color, perhaps H, and its clarity is SI,

et al.

indicative of imperfections. This diamond weighs just 19.45 carats. It is a valuable stone and captures a lot of light, but not worth more than one fifth the value of the Steinhart diamond. Also, I recognize the jeweler's mark engraved in the setting - The Happy Sunshine Jewelry Company in Hong Kong."

"What does all that mean?" asked the captain.

"Maybe one of the crew took the ring, after all," said Helen. "But they didn't take the Steinhart diamond."

"It's unlikely the crew would have obtained this substitute for the real thing," said Mr. Sicher. "First of all, Mrs. Vogel would have recognized the switch in a heartbeat. That just would not have worked. Secondly, it would have taken more money than crew members have to buy the substitute. So one of the crew must have thought he or she was stealing the real thing."

"And conscience pangs must have prompted the return," said the captain.

"It seems likely to me that a crew member stole this ring from a person or persons trying to commit insurance fraud," said Mr. Sicher. "The perps probably wanted to confuse investigators about where and when the real ring went missing. Some confederate onboard probably was supposed to take a handoff of the fake."

Helen rose from her chair. "I'll check the passenger list to look for a possible accomplice."

The others waited for Helen to return. She returned minutes later. "Look who I found. Yin Huang boarded in Hong Kong and left the ship in Singapore, just like the Vogels. And he worked for The Happy Sunshine Jewelry Company."

"Do you have his passport number?" asked Mr. Sicher.

"Right here," said Helen.

"I'll notify the authorities," said Mr. Sicher. "They will question Mr. Huang and officials at the jewelry store. The substitute ring will be important evidence in an insurance fraud case. When do you reach a U.S. port?"

"We arrive in Fort Lauderdale April thirtieth," said the captain.

"Please keep the ring in your safe until you get to Fort Lauderdale. Law enforcement might be involved. I'm sure you will be notified."

RICHARD SICHER AND MICHAEL Stern left the ship and took an airplane to San Francisco, the headquarters for TransAmerica. Sicher took a deposition from Michael Stern regarding his findings and filed a report. Then he called the Vogel home.

"John Vogel speaking."

"Hello Mr. Vogel. This is Richard Sicher from TransAmerica. Remember me?"

et al.

"Sure do. How are things going? Did you bring our ring back from the ship?"

"Turned out it wasn't the ring you claimed the loss on. Looked very much like it, but was worth only a small fraction of your ring's value. What do you think of that?"

"What? How can that be? I just don't get it."

"The people at TransAmerica don't get it, either. How could a ring that looked like the one you lost turn up on the ship? Also, it is very strange that no one seems to claim this new ring. Any ideas?"

"No, you've got me stumped."

"Is Mrs. Vogel there?"

"No, she went to Hong Kong. I know she is very concerned about her ring, but she's still trying to raise money with Sam Lieu for our new startup, and they have reached a critical phase. I'll give you her email address."

THE SHIP SAILED ON as planned. She passed through the Suez Canal and the Mediterranean. On April 13, after stopping at many ports along the way, she reached Athens to once again disgorge many passengers and take on new ones.

Part Four

FATHER JIM COLLINS APPEARED at the door of Captain Derek's office. "I have to have an important meeting with you, Captain."

"Come on in, Father. What can I do for you?"

The priest shut the door and sat down across the desk from the captain. "It's a long story, Captain, and a sad one."

"Go ahead, Father."

"You may or may not know that Samu Gandhi and Monica Felipe are romantically involved. Some time ago they asked me for my advice about getting married. I told them that love alone is not enough for a successful marriage. They are of different races, from different countries, and they still have close ties to their villages and families. I said it would be really difficult for one of them to totally give up the life they are used to for the other's culture."

"Sounds realistic, Father."

"But here is where my logic may not have been helpful. I said if they could travel back and forth between their homelands, it could enable each of them to keep touch with their roots, and that could make their marriage happier. Maybe they could keep one home in each of their countries."

"Nothing really wrong with that advice, either."

et al.

"But, I explained, that would require significant money. I asked how much they had saved between them. Captain, they only have four thousand dollars. Do you know how much they might need? At least one hundred thousand dollars and more would be better. That would take them many years to save. So I advised them to forget marriage barring some kind of miracle."

"A sad tale, but probably a sound conclusion."

"Captain, they took the ring. Monica saw Mrs. Vogel put the ring in the vanity drawer, she told Samu, and he took it when he delivered the hors d'oevures to the suite. Samu has contacts in Calcutta who could dispose of the ring for him, and they would have become fabulously wealthy. Don't you see? They could get married. Love made them do it."

"Love makes people do crazy things, doesn't it, Father?"

"They came to me in tears a week after they took the ring, and both have confessed their sins. They are at peace with God. They also dictated this confession, which I have here. They are ashamed and couldn't face you."

With that, Father Jim handed over a written confession signed by the lovers. "I'm afraid my advice may have led them to this deed, so I feel some guilt. Can't you cut them some slack?"

Rolf's brow wrinkled. *What can I do? The young couple was overcome by temptation. Who is this sinner to judge others?* "There's not too much I can do for them. I will ask the Crew

Manager to terminate them immediately. Their employment record will have to point out the theft. Sorry, that's all I can do. I hope they will be able to get new jobs."

"They already left the ship this morning in Athens. Will there be criminal charges brought?"

"I don't know who would bring them. The Vogels claim to know nothing of the ring, and if they change their minds, that would implicate them in fraud. So I don't think Monica and Samu have anything to fear along those lines. And their theft may have foiled a fraud attempt. At least the insurance company will be happy with this news," the captain said, "This places possession of the substitute ring with the Vogels." He sent a confidential fax copy of the confession to Richard Sicher.

After receiving the faxed report from the *Seafarer*, Richard couldn't wait to hear John Vogel's response to the news.

"Mr. Vogel, this is Richard Sicher, TransAmerica, again. Do you have a moment?"

"Yes. Did you contact my wife? I have been trying to reach her myself."

"No, she hasn't answered my emails."

"Do you have any information about our missing ring?"

"Just this. Two crew members have confessed to taking the ring, the one you and your wife knew nothing about, from your

et al.

suite. And one other thing. We traced the jeweler's mark in the setting to a company in Hong Kong, The Happy Sunshine Jewelry Company."

"My God, Sylvia and I visited there when we were in Hong Kong."

"Interesting."

"Mr. Sicher, I think I've been played for a fool. Let's get this thing settled so I can get on with my life. My life with Sylvia may be over."

The *Seafarer* went out into the Atlantic and crossed westward. After a two quick stops in the Caribbean Islands she reached Fort Lauderdale. Sicher came aboard. "Let's go to my office," suggested the captain. "Helen and Sven are already there."

When they were seated, Mr. Sicher began, "Well, I think everything has been settled in an amazingly short time. Your cruise company is cleared of all liability."

"Thank God," said Rolf. "I should be able to keep my job."

Sicher continued, "The Vogel's were in a hurry to settle, so time was on our side. Mrs. Vogel maintained her ring was gone and she had no idea where that ring on your desk came from. She signed a disclaimer of ownership for the substitute. She eventually fell silent.

"Here was the real breakthrough. The authorities got possession of her personal computer. She thought she had deleted her files, but she didn't realize they are never really gone, and the police in Hong Kong had all the scheming and agreements of Mrs. Vogel, Sam Lieu, and the jewelry store on her hard drive." Sicher continued, emphasizing each important point.

* "Sylvia and Sam kept their plans secret from Mr. Vogel, who was not involved. The poor guy was not in their plans for the new company.

* "The jewelry store wanted the ring to go missing far away from Hong Kong. The authorities were making it hot for them locally.

* "The substitute had to closely resemble the Steinhart diamond. Many passengers would recognize a replica, let alone a shift to cubic zirconia. Besides, at the appropriate time, Sylvia was to hand off the fake to Mr. Huang. So there wasn't a large risk."

* The Vogels dropped their insurance claim, Sylvia to avoid a fraud charge and John in exchange for TransAmerica's dropping any claim to the ring."

"We heard that Mr. Vogel is back working with DoubleTalk? What happened to Mrs. Vogel?" asked the captain.

"She is still working with Sam Lieu. They proposed a new startup, CrazyTalk, and they were promised seed funding of

et al.

$15M from unnamed Hong Kong investors. That was called off because of the Steinhart diamond fraud. The authorities are still trying to find out what happened to the ring.

"By the way, the Vogels are no longer married. Mr. Vogel filed for divorce in Las Vegas, and Mrs. Vogel flew there to complete the transaction."

"Then who owns the substitute ring," asked Sven.

"Mrs. Vogel disclaimed ownership, so that makes Mr. Vogel its owner in my book. It was stolen from his cabin. Mr. Vogel will get possession of the ring and should be able to sell it for four or five million dollars. That cash along with a raft of repos should be enough to satisfy their creditors."

"John Vogel is out a twenty-three-million-dollar ring, and he lost a wife. I feel sorry for him," said Helen.

" I don't know," said the captain. "In some ways I think he was the luckiest of the characters in this fiasco."

Night at the
Westerville Lodge

I WAS SHOT AND killed in a field near the place people call Westerville, Iowa. My body was disassembled and much of me was reassembled with wire and oakum, and I was placed in a display case here at the lodge. I can neither see through these glass eyes nor hear through these propped-up ears, but my spirit has decided to hang around here together with the majority of my worldly residue enclosed by my white fur. I can feel and sense presences and thoughts even though, much as I would like, I can't physically interact with the world.

A couple of hunters are coming through the front door. They are being met by the owner, the guy who killed me.

"HI, BRIAN DEEMER HERE. Welcome to Westerville Lodge. You must be Mike Daughton. And this is your son, James?"

et al.

"Hi Brian, good to meet you. Where should we put our stuff?"

"You two got the back bedroom. Tonight, you're the only guests. Just throw your sleeping bags on the cots. There are spare blankets if you need them. Have you eaten?"

"Yeah. James and I ate on the road."

"I have rolls out for your breakfast and the coffee maker is already loaded. In the morning you will find a lunch sack with deer sausage sandwiches and oranges in the fridge.

"Dad, look at all the deer heads on the wall. There are one, two...seven of them. What antlers!"

"Yes," says Brian. "These are all trophies. Nothing on the wall measures less than 200."

"What does that mean?" asks James.

"Standard Boone and Crocket measurements for antlers." Mike says. "The ratings are a little complicated, but it's basically the inches of horn in the rack."

"This new one here measures 210. James, we call it a twelve-pointer because there are six horn points on each antler," says Brian.

"My, my. What's this in the glass case under the TV?" asks Mike.

"That's a male white coyote. I shot him on a hunt last March. We shot his parents and all their siblings, too."

"Must be an albino," muses Mike.

"Nope. Just a rare product of recessive genes. He's about one in 100,000. His brothers and sisters were white, too, but both parents were normal coyote colors."

"Boy this one sure looks realistic," says James.

"That's a fantastic job of mounting," says Mike.

"Yep, I was pleased with the way he's at attention, his front paws up on that stump. He's looking out into the distance, alerted to some sound or movement."

"Who painted the background?" asks Mike.

"My sister painted the winter-night scene. It looks okay in the daytime, but at night, wow! It really comes to life with the lights off. I put in a black light that makes everything glow purple in a dark room, that moon especially."

THEY'RE TALKING ABOUT ME now, I can feel it. How I was hunted down with the rest of my family by all those hunters. And by those nasty dogs, those traitors to the canine family. I don't understand why they wanted to kill us. There weren't enough of us to piece together a decent coyote fur coat. We aren't human food. We didn't bother their cattle. We just killed and ate mice and rabbits.

et al.

My parents taught me to hunt. We had to eat. There was nothing personal about killing. We weren't like the feline family. Cats enjoy playing with cripples until finally tiring of the sport and dispatching their victims.

Humans are carnivorous just like us. Consider their canine teeth. They don't enjoy killing like cats. Their ancient forbears just hunted for food, but today's humans like to celebrate their achievements in hunting. Deer heads on the wall are a way of remembering. They are trophies. I'm one, too.

"WHAT'S THAT THING UNDER the table?" asks Mike.

"That's my iRobot sweeper in a docking station. I'll show you what it can do when I press this button. First comes the cavalry charge music, and now the action."

"God, it really charges across the floor," says James.

"Yep, in a straight line until it hits something," says Brian. "Then it tracks off into a different direction."

"Is it heavy?" asks Mike.

"Go ahead and lift it," says Brian. "You won't hurt anything."

"Pretty heavy for something a little bigger that a dinner plate," says Mike. "What happens when its battery runs down?"

"It senses when it's time to go back to the docking station for a recharge. I set a timer for it to work in the mornings. Haven't had to sweep this place for a month."

"I've never seen anything like this before," says James. "I'd like to just sit here a while and watch it work."

"I have the only one in the county," says Brian. "It's my pride and joy. Visitors from all over the county stop by to see it."

"My," says James. "Has it got a brain? It seems so intelligent."

"No, James," says Brian. "It's just programmed to do what it does. It's just a dumb machine."

"I suppose James and I should hit the hay pretty soon," says Mike.

"What kind of licenses do you have?" asks Brian.

"We can take one buck and one doe," says Mike. "I'm hoping one of us can bag a buck with a rack like those on the wall. And we'll take a doe for eating."

"Yeah, bucks just after the rut are worn out from fighting and chasing does. You've got to grind them up with beef and pork fat and lots of spices," says Brian.

"With sugar and especially lots of red pepper," says Mike.

"I'll shut down the robot, so it won't bother your sleep," says Brian. "Now get some shut-eye so you'll be fresh for the hunt in the morning."

et al.

AH, HERE COMES THE son. It's still the middle of the night. He's stretching out in a recliner facing my glass cage. He peers into my case glowing violet in a midnight winter scene. He sees me, an inanimate object once full of life.

The boy is thinking about a wonderful day in the deer stand. He's seeing a big buck, roaming wild in the woods. A twelve-pointer, maybe a fourteen-pointer. He sights the heart area through the scope. Should he pull the trigger? This magnificent creature roaming wild and free. Should the stag die so he can put a head in his bedroom? There may be some benefit in the bad-tasting sausage stored in the freezer for years. But killing the beast just doesn't feel right to him.

What would his dad think about this? He would say the buck wouldn't live forever, anyway. And the trophy is a symbol that will bring back memories of the outdoors and hunting when you are cooped up at work or school. And it symbolizes success, something you did well.

Here comes that iRobot thing. It'll wake everyone. After it breaks permanently, the owner may mount the damned thing next to the deer heads. Here comes the father rubbing his eyes and turning on the coffee maker.

"HOW COME YOU ARE out here this morning, Son?"

"I dunno. Just couldn't sleep. Maybe I'm too excited."

"James, you'd better get dressed for cold weather. Have a couple of rolls and some milk."

"All set?" asks Brian as he comes from a back bedroom. "What are you hunting with?"

"I'm letting James use my 20 gauge with rifled slugs. I've got a black powder rifle, effective range of a hundred fifty yards."

"Good luck on the hunt," says Brian. "Hope you get a trophy buck."

THERE THEY GO, OFF to hunt just like their human ancestors. I like the boy. He was asking the right questions. But given a chance he will kill a big buck. He can't help it. It's in his genes.

Her Majesty's Birthday Note

To my executors: This extraordinary tale, documented here by Dr. John Watson, must not become public until the start of the third millennium. By then it is hoped the public will be more understanding and considerate of a lonely widow with the weight of the Empire on her shoulders.

—S. Holmes

December 10, 1881

*O*N A COLD, FOGGY winter morning in London, I heard a rapping on the front door of our residence on Baker Street. Mrs. Hudson led two men up the stairs to 221 B and took their black capes used to shelter them from the elements.

et al.

"Please see to it we are not disturbed, Mrs. Hudson," said Sherlock Holmes. He shut the door to our flat as she left.

"Dr. Watson, you already know my brother, Mycroft. And this is John Brown, a trusted servant to the Queen."

I shook hands with a tall, well-built man who wore black and red kilts of his clan. His ruddy complexion suggested a life outdoors. Muttonchops on his jowls framed a rectangular face.

"Pleased to meet you Dr. Watson." He stood warming his backside toward our fireplace.

"Good to see you again, Doctor," said Mycroft. "You seem to be taking good care of my little brother."

Mycroft was pale and overweight due to physical indolence, but a mighty intelligence stared out from gray eyes that lay beneath his overgrown eyebrows.

"I do my best, sir," I replied.

Sherlock seemed impatient to get to the point. "Let us sit around our table. As I understand from my brother, we have an extremely urgent matter to discuss involving Her Majesty and the Empire," said Sherlock.

"Before we begin, I have a concern," said Brown. "Not to offend Dr. Watson, but is he absolutely trustworthy? This is a very sensitive matter."

"No one has ever questioned my loyalty or discretion before, but I'll step outside if you desire," I said.

"Please stay, Watson. Gentlemen, I would and do trust this man with my life," said Sherlock.

"And you may have to do that in this matter," said Mycroft.

We took seats each on one side of a small, square table. There was an awkward silence. John Brown was first to speak. "This was all my fault. Her Majesty wrote me a note the morning of December 8th wishing me a happy birthday, and one of the servants, we're still trying to discover which one, took the note from my desk. I should have locked it away."

"What could possibly be wrong with a birthday wish from our good Queen Victoria?" asked Dr. Watson.

John Brown's face turned two shades redder than its normal ruddy color. "Oh, god. This is so embarrassing. Her Majesty suggested what she had planned for that night, and oh my, if the note were public..." His chin fell to his chest as he heaved a sigh. A tear showed at the corner of each eye.

"And so the note suggests behavior unbecoming the Queen?" asked Sherlock.

"I'm afraid many would think so," said Brown. "I have asked her to marry me and have given her my mother's wedding ring. But she has worn black this past twenty years since Albert died.

et al.

He was the love of her life and she would do nothing to detract from her first marriage."

"This has become more than a matter of the heart," said Mycroft. "Here is how the government has become involved. Somehow the note has fallen into the hands of a political group opposing liberalization of tenant laws in Ireland."

"Bloody Irish," said Holmes. "They are never satisfied. They breed like rabbits. Seems like the landowners are always giving, but it's never enough."

"Well, I can tell you," said Mr. Brown, "that our Queen is sympathetic with the Irish peasant. Since the potato famine over two million of the poor beggars have died from disease and starvation, and two million more have had to emigrate. Her Majesty supports the additional reforms."

"Whitehall assigned me to retrieve or destroy that note," said Mycroft. "A group of wealthy landowners want to blackmail Queen Victoria into opposing reforms and Irish Home Rule. And they want a public proclamation from her to that effect."

John Brown said, "Our William Gladstone is quietly working with an Irish leader by the name of Charles Parnell, a prisoner in Kilmainham Jail. The Prime Minister and Parnell seem to be making rapid progress toward solving, or at least ameliorating, the tenant problems. Parnell is a landowner and a Protestant, a most peculiar man."

"A traitor to his kind," said Holmes.

"We must get that note back to protect Queen Victoria," said Brown.

"And to prevent interference in our Irish affairs," added Mycroft.

"Well," asked Sherlock, "what is to be done?"

"I have arranged a meeting with a representative of the group holding the note," said Mycroft. "I have demanded an opportunity for a handwriting expert - that's you, Sherlock - to review the document in order to verify its authenticity. You must use your wit to somehow destroy the note. Watson should go with you. I am forewarning you. Your lives may be in danger. These are rough people."

"Do you still have your revolver from your India service, Watson?" asked Sherlock.

"I do indeed. I have my trusty Adams," I said.

"I must accept the challenge," said Holmes. "I require a note in the Queen's hand, so I might be familiar with it."

John Brown removed a note from his pouch. "This blue envelope contains a note from the Queen. It's very similar to the note in question, but it's far less controversial."

"Good," said Holmes. "I also require a quill and ink Her Majesty uses."

et al.

"That will be sent by messenger as soon as I return to Buckingham," said Brown.

THAT AFTERNOON THE QUILL and ink arrived, and Holmes set to work studying the note that Brown had left. All through the evening into the small hours of the morning Sherlock scratched out lines, characters, and sentences on the Queen's notepaper using one of her quills. We had a short sleep and just a quick cup of tea in the morning when it was time to go to the rendezvous at the East End address that Mycroft gave us. I carried the articles Holmes was to use to authenticate the note: a quill, ink, and blank notepaper Her Majesty used, and a note in her hand. We climbed into the carriage on a cold day with the sun occasionally peaking between dark clouds racing across the sky, and we proceeded toward our appointment with our single horse's hooves clip-clomping on the pavement.

"Holmes, I didn't know you had an interest in handwriting," I remarked.

"My dear Watson, after publishing a few monographs on the subject, I was appointed a Professor of Graphology at Cambridge."

"You never cease to amaze me."

"It's not such a difficult science. But I have to say I've never seen such an unusual writing as our Queen's. Her vertical strokes are unusually long and narrow and are slanted right at an exaggerated angle. To complicate it further, there are clear traces of German script in her flourishes and swirls because she wrote first in that language as a child. I have to say, her note was difficult to read."

Our carriage drove to the Thames and then along a street lined with warehouses. Uncollected horse droppings covered the cobblestones and emitted an unpleasant odor. Coal smoke blackened the buildings and garbage piles punctuated the walkways. Our cabby pulled up at our meeting place, a nondescript warehouse.

"It's now 10:00," said Holmes to our driver. "Please be here promptly at 11:00 to return us to Baker Street."

We climbed a short set of stairs and Holmes knocked. The door opened, and a giant of a man appeared. He wore a tweed coat over a pullover sweater, and his muscular body seemed struggling to break the bonds of his clothing. He wore a stocking cap pulled down over his ears. "Professor Holmes?" he asked.

"Yes," said Sherlock. "And this is my assistant, Dr. Watson."

"Step in," the big man commanded.

We stepped inside, and a smaller man came out from behind the door. His brown and wrinkled face, pug nose, long ears, and slicked down black hair reminded me of a rabbit. He held a revolver and took turns pointing at Holmes and me. He relieved

et al.

me of my own weapon and motioned with his gun for us to climb a flight of stairs. A room at the top held a table with two chairs and a table with an oil lamp burning dimly at its center. Next to the lamp was a light blue envelope. It was cold in the room, and we chose to keep our coats and hats on.

"The note is in the envelope. No funny stuff," said the gunman. "I'll be watching you like a hawk."

"I require some tools of my trade," said Sherlock. "I will need to examine the note you claim to be written by the Queen, and to compare it with one I have brought here. Also, I have a magnifying glass and some writing materials with which to make notes. We will keep them on the table, but at one end. Will that be acceptable?"

The gunman looked across the dimly lit room, and I saw for the first time a stark, white face staring out from a black cloak that shrouded a man and the chair he was sitting on. He frowned, but nodded up and down, indicating we could put the materials on the table.

Holmes got down to work. He removed the note from the blue envelope and viewed it under a magnifying glass. He then did the same with the note we had put on the table. He repeated this many times, and after each observation he wrote with the Queen's quill and compared the ink traces with that of the note in question.

Suddenly there was a loud pounding on the front door. "Open up, Scotland Yard," commanded a voice downstairs.

The gunman drew his revolver and went to the head of the stairs. The giant downstairs opened the door. "What seems to be the problem, officer?"

"An escaped prisoner has been seen in this area. Have you seen anything suspicious?"

"No sir. I am the watchman at this warehouse, and last night and this morning have been very quiet here."

"Sorry to bother you. But if you see or hear anything suspicious, be sure to notify us."

"I certainly will, officer," said the watchman, and he shut the door. The gunman at the head of the stairs went back to his post and stared at the table, Holmes, and me.

Sherlock continued with his work, comparing the two notes under a magnifying glass and making notes. Finally, he returned the note to the blue envelope and set it by the lamp. He gathered our materials and was about to put them in our satchel when the gunman said, "Not so fast. I want to examine those materials."

"Certainly," said Holmes.

The gunman examined the Queen's note we had brought. "Thought you might have tried to exchange this for our note, but I see it's dated last summer."

et al.

He then opened the blue envelope and examined the note it contained. He seemed satisfied.

"May we go now?" asked Sherlock.

"First, I have to frisk you," said the gunman. He patted us down thoroughly.

"Would you please return my weapon?" I asked.

"Yes, here you are." He returned my gun, but with all the cartridges removed.

The mysterious white face in the corner asked, "What are your findings, Professor Holmes?"

"You may tell your employer that your note is authentic."

Holmes and I walked down the stairs, out through the front door where the giant stood, and down the steps to the waiting carriage. I checked my watch, and it read 11:00. "Goodness, Holmes, you surely had this timed exactly."

"It is probably expedient for us to be gone is quickly as possible," said Holmes. "That man in the upstairs corner was Professor James Moriority. He is evil incarnate, a very dangerous character."

"It is unfortunate we were unable to destroy the Queen's note," I said.

"We may still be able to do so," said Holmes.

Puzzled as to how that was to be accomplished, I rode back to 222 Baker Street. Sherlock offered no further explanation. Mrs. Hudson brought us a pot of tea and some biscuits as we sat by the fire.

"WELL, SIR, HOW ARE we to destroy the note while it is still in the hands of those villains over on the East End?" I asked.

"They do have a note," said Sherlock, "But it is one written in my own hand."

"How can that possibly be?" I exclaimed.

"I fancy I can emulate the Queen's writing pretty well, and I wrote a note very much like the one of interest during my examination. When the scoundrels were distracted by the Scotland Yard, I replaced the real note with my own."

"Did you know they would pound on the door?"

"Yes, I have a good friend there, a P. Lestrade. He was to knock at 10:45."

"But we were searched. Where is the note?"

"Perhaps it is under the earflap of this herringbone hat." Holmes undid the bow holding the flaps on top and pulled out a note. It may prove instructive for you to hear the contents. He read aloud.

December 8, 1862

Buckingham Castle

My Darling John,

The Queen wishes you a very happy birthday, and thanks you for your years of dedicated service. You have been a valuable confidant during the day and even more so at night when we lay together in bed. Then I can put all the problems of my station on your broad shoulders and my burdens are lightened.

Tonight, I would like to repay you in my small way by giving my stallion a wild ride he will not soon forget.

Victoria, RI

"MY, OH MY. THAT is a very suggestive note," I said. "Who would expect such from a sixty-two-year-old widow in mourning?"

"Well, Doctor, she did have eight children with Albert. She may still possess some of the same urges she had when younger."

"And what did the note you wrote say?"

"I am rather proud that my own note replaced only six words from the original with five of my own. To casual observation the two notes look alike, almost line for line. And with Victoria's difficult handwriting it was easy to pass off my note as the Queen's."

Holmes recited his forgery from memory. I had underlined here the four words different from the original.

December 8, 1862

Buckingham Castle

My Darling John,

The Queen wishes you a very happy birthday, and thanks you for your years of dedicated service. You are a valued confidant during the day and even more so at night when we <u>eat</u> together <u>at six</u>. Then I can put all the problems of my station on your broad shoulders, and my burdens are lightened.

Tonight, I would like to repay you in my small way by giving my <u>stalwart</u> a <u>whisky</u> he will not soon forget.

Victoria, RI

I REMARKED, "THE NOTE the crooks have seems just like a nice thank you note from the Queen."

"Yes, but it's a forgery. What do you think we should do with the note we have?"

"It should be destroyed," I said. "Its life should end in our fireplace."

"I hope in the future our royalty can behave like real people and not be so constrained by the artificial boundaries we place around them," said Sherlock.

Holmes threw the note in the fireplace and it soon went up in flames along with the chance for Irish landlords to blackmail the Queen into doing their bidding.

The Nemesis

*D*AVID JOHNSON SET THE plate with what remained of his breakfast on the counter. His wife said, "Dear, you just pick at your food and hardly sleep. I suppose you're worried about this tenure thing".

"Yeah, and today the committee reports to the department chair. Without a positive recommendation, my six-year teaching career here at State ends, and so will job prospects at any other respectable institution."

"If the worst happens, we'll manage. We'll still be able to keep our little family together."

"Marge, nice of you to be so positive. We can barely manage our current mortgage, and when our third kid comes this summer, this two-bedroom house will be too small. A job change will require a move, an expensive proposition. We really do have a lot riding on the decision. With tenure, our credit would be golden, and a higher mortgage would not be a problem."

et al.

David dressed like an associate professor; Scottish tweed sport coat with leather elbow pads, white button-down shirt without a necktie, black horn-rim glasses, and Birkenstock sandals without socks.

"You look great," said Marge.

They hugged and then kissed. "The baby bump is getting between us," said Dave.

"Good luck with the tenure committee," said Marge.

He drove his Volkswagen Bug to the student union, took the elevator to the top floor, and entered the Faculty Lounge. His friend, colleague, and Assistant Professor, Buzz Smith, waited for him at a quiet table in the rear.

They exchanged greetings and ordered coffee. Then Buzz said, "Big day today, huh Dave?"

"Indeed, and I'm both worried and a little scared. I see my tenure committee is meeting across the dining room. Looks like they're having a good, old time. Well, it isn't their ass on the line. They have spent three months compiling my life story: academic record, theses, publications, student feedback, and faculty relations. They did the same thing exactly three years ago, half the six-year tenure determination period."

"You and I come from a solid-state physics background, unusual for an electrical engineering department," said Buzz. "But that's the wave of the future."

"Yeah," said Dave. "And many of the old professors over there don't even believe in transistor memories. They like motors, generators, and vacuum tubes."

"Do you think the committee might hold your field of expertise against you for tenure? You might think it would be a plus, might get the department into the twentieth century."

"It could actually be a problem. You attended some of the donnybrooks between Dr. Krowder and me in faculty meetings. It got almost personal a few times. He understands inductive sensors and doesn't believe that spin-transport devices will ever replace them. Krowder might blackball me in the meeting. That's my biggest worry."

Buzz said, "It doesn't help anything that you backed into Krowder's car last month, that brand new Cadillac. It was his pride and joy."

"No, it doesn't. I told him I was sorry and was willing to pay for fixing the damages. He told his friends, 'I had a new Cad, but after it comes out of the shop, it will be just a repaired wreck.'"

Hans Krowder, sitting at the table with others on the tenure committee, waved at us. White muttonchops adorned the sides of his ruddy face. He wore a double-breasted, navy-blue suit, a red tie on a white shirt, and black dress shoes polished to a high gloss. What was he thinking? Was it 'Happy to see you this morning on your big day,' or was it 'Now I've got you, you son-of-a-bitch!'?

et al.

Buzz said, "Gotta go back to the office and grade finals. You done with yours?"

"Yes, I finished yesterday and turned in grades for both my classes. I'll go to my office and await the call from the department head. He meets with the committee until 11:30 and should discuss the verdict with me by noon."

Back in the office Dave had a phone voice message, "No matter what happens, honey, everything will work out. Love you. Your life partner, Marge."

Dave looked at ads in *Electronic News* for positions available. No job excited his interest. He perused the *Proceeding of the 1985 Magnetics Conference*. Time passed slowly. Finally, just before noon, the telephone rang. "Dave, would you please come to my office," said the department head.

He walked along a long hall, his heart rattling his rib cage. The office door was open, and Professor Warren Boast invited him in and then shut the door. Dave sat across the desk from him.

"I know you are anxious to learn the committee's recommendation, so here goes. You were recommended for tenure by our department. Your tenure will almost certainly be rubber-stamped by the dean and president, they always approve. You will have a job here, Dave, so long as you don't grievously mess up. Congratulations."

Dave released a long, shaking sigh, and took a few seconds to get his breath back. "Thank you so much, Dr. Boast. I can't tell you how relieved I feel."

"Do you have any questions? I sat through the entire meeting this morning."

"Were there any in opposition to granting tenure?"

"I'm not supposed to disclose individual interactions, but I will mention something about technical judgment. Remember three years ago at your preliminary review? Some thought you weren't realistic about new technology and its practical value."

"Yes, I remember."

"Well, it came up again this morning. The discussion got quite heated. One person argued powerfully in your defense. He said the department needed to cope with new technology, and your tenure was a start. You had a real advocate."

"Could you tell who that person was?"

"I'm not supposed to disclose personal opinions in the meeting. But if you swear on a stack of bibles you won't tell anyone, I'll give you a hint."

"All right, I swear."

"At the start of the meeting, he said his Cadillac was good as new."

Rhymes with Orange

"When I use a word,' Humpty Dumpty said in rather a scornful tone, 'it means just what I choose it to mean— neither more nor less.'

'The question is,' said Alice, 'whether you can make words mean so many different things.'

'The question is,' said Humpty Dumpty, 'which is to be master—that's all."

Lewis Carroll, Through the Looking Glass

et al.

Littleton Junior College
Room 5
Littleton, Arkansas 71503

Oxford University Press   July 18, 2018
Great Clarendon Street
Oxford OX2 6DP
United Kingdom

Dear Ms Goodword:

As I understand it, your distinguished *Oxford English Dictionary* accepts, after thorough reviews, new words each year. I am proposing several new words for next year's edition.

I have taught remedial English for seventeen years here at Littleton and believe me when I say student essays have supplied me with countless words not in your dictionary, nor should they ever be. The new words I propose seek to right a wrong done the word orange. There seems to be no word in your dictionary that is its full and proper rhyme.

I propose five new words that rhyme with orange.

- Forange – Verb meaning to forage on rangeland.
- Morange – Morning during sunrise when the sky is reddish-yellow.
- Porange – A mixture of Tang and oatmeal used for a fast, nutritious breakfast in space.
- Storange – To store and arrange at the same time.
- Gorange – To eat way too many oranges.

To see how easily these kinds of words can be used in poetry, consider the following examples. As background, an astronaut retires to a ranch in Montana. He turns his herd out to graze in the early morning at sunrise. He sits in the early sun, answers his mail, and then eats the breakfast he got used to in space.

To wit:

*A rancher sent his herd to **forange***
*On a bright and sunny **morange**.*
He sat back and basked,
Answered questions he's asked,
*And polished off a big bowl of **porange**.*

Or the greedy gourmand:

*To a platter from a basket he **storanges***
A very large pile of oranges.
He consumes them all down,
But then said with a frown,
*"This is my last time for **goranges**."*

et al.

Please consider my word suggestions. Perhaps your committees can come up with even more suitable words. My biggest concern is that *orange* gets a fair shake.

Sincerely Yours,

Armer Judge

Armer Judge

Instructor

Section B:

Growing Up &

Growing Old

Christmas 1946

December 23

A CALL FROM NATURE awakened her. Kay rolled to her right and reached out with her left arm. No Dwain. That's right, he won't be home until this evening. So much to do in the next three days. At least I don't have to teach during vacation. I hope I can make this first Christmas since the war the best holiday ever for our family, even under these difficult conditions. I especially hope Dwain likes his suitcase.

She recalled a letter her husband had sent from somewhere in the Pacific as the war had neared its end in 1945.

> *"I'm afraid we will have a rough time when I get home. Five million returning servicemen and seven million war workers should pretty well swamp the labor market. I'll need clothes, a car, and money to get around looking for a job. I hope you've saved a little something, so I won't have to take a job digging ditches somewhere."*

et al.

Unfortunately, she hadn't saved much from her allotment, which was barely adequate for her and three kids. Dwain was not pleased. And in another letter, he had written,

> *"I wish we had bought some cheap acreage around Grand River, so we would have had some place to go where we wouldn't have to pay rent and could live cheaply during our transition period."*

So that's how they ended up a mile from Grand River, Iowa in a tiny house without running water, not even drinkable water, no electricity, and no central heating. Dwain's father and mother, Alice and Emmett, lived in Grand River and lent him the $2500 for the house, outbuildings, and six acres of land. He got a job with the Veterans Administration that required him to travel all week in southwest Iowa mentoring disabled veterans in training programs. She and Dwain had saved enough in ten months to buy an oil-furnace to heat the house, and a propane stove for the kitchen. Kay taught half time—music to all thirteen grades and English to high school seniors. Her salary was $100 per month. She turned over her paychecks to Dwain.

Kay rolled out of bed, pulled a robe on over her pajamas, and stepped into slippers. She lit a Camel and took a long drag and grabbed the flashlight. A blast of cold air greeted her as she opened the back door to the porch. She donned a coat and boots and stepped through the porch door to face the elements. It was calm. Light snow deadened all sound. It wasn't the heavy, blanketing snow she wanted for a white Christmas, but at least it partially covered dead grass. The eastern sky gave scant promise for a sunrise. She dreaded the walk past the fruit cave, the picket fence, the burn barrel, the clothesline, and the chicken yard to the two-hole, brick and stucco outhouse, but she dreaded even more the thought of sitting down on a cold wood toilet seat. Pine Sol, lime, and the cold combined to deaden the smell of human waste. She lifted one of the wooden hole-covers. Its underside was smothered with hoar frost. She remembered Macbeth's agonizing before killing Duncan. "If it were when 'tis done, then 'twere well it were done quickly." And she finished the business that brought her there.

On her way back, she flicked her cigarette butt into the burn barrel, then put away her boots and hung up her coat on the porch. She needed the flashlight to find a box of matches, so she could light the gas lamp, being careful not to touch the mantle. They were so fragile, and they cost five cents apiece. Then there was light enough to fill the coffee pot from the water pail and set it on the stove. She took out her teeth and brushed them. She never wanted to be seen without her teeth, especially not by Dwain. The damned dentist in Creston has persuaded her to pull them all. "Better to be done with it rather than being nickeled and dimed to death by cavities."

Emmett and Alice had a good well, so Dwain hauled a ten-gallon cream can of their water to the back porch every week. A dipper sat in a two-gallon bucket of that water on the kitchen counter. Next to the sink, a small hand pump was used to draw water from the cistern. Although it was contaminated, after boiling, it could be used to wash dishes. Kay filled the teakettle and sat it on a burner beside the coffee pot.

The house was cold, so Kay turned the oil stove up to six, the highest level. She moved the kettle of pork neck-bones and vegetables to a cooler spot; they were probably done already. The seven o'clock whistle blew in Grand River, a mile away. Soon the coffee pot was perking. She turned on the battery radio. "This is H.V. Kaltenborn with the first network news analysis of the day." The three kids got up, hugged their mother, and hovered as close to the stove as possible without scorching their pajamas.

"What's for breakfast, Mom?" asked Jim.

"Cheerios and bananas with milk. There's tomato juice, too. If anyone wants toast, I'll make some. We have cherry jam."

All three wanted toast. So she turned on a burner and held pieces of bread on a fork over the flames. In a few minutes she had some partially charred toast on a plate.

They ate a quiet breakfast. "Your father is coming home this evening. He'll be tired after a week on the road, so let's be on our best behavior. Now it's getting light enough to do your chores. Take the slop bucket to the pigs and the wastebasket to the burn barrel."

Jim's major job was to milk Bossy. Kay was glad to turn that job over to her oldest. Now that he had turned ten, he was a big help. He was just barely strong enough to pump water from their well for the stock tank. Unfortunately, that water tasted too bad for humans, but the animals didn't seem to mind it.

Bruce at age eight fed and watered the chickens and pigs. He had to carry water in a three-gallon bucket from the stock tank to pig troughs and automatic chicken waterers.

Sheila, aged six, picked up the dishes and washed them. Her main chore was to gather eggs. She would wait until mid-morning when the chickens would be done with their duties.

Jim brought in two and a half gallons of milk. Kay reserved a couple of quarts for drinking, then strained the remaining milk through cheesecloth into a gravity separator and added another gallon of water. Cream would rise to the top. And in a few hours the spigot at the bottom could be opened, and a water/milk mix would flow into a five-gallon bucket. Later, pigs would enjoy the contents from the pig trough. When cream would start to flow instead, the remainder would be poured into a gallon cream bucket. Some of it would be saved for home use, and the rest would be taken to town on Saturday to be sold. Dwain let her have that money to spend as she chose, about three dollars a week.

The telephone mounted on the wall rang a long and three shorts. Kay and about six others on the party line lifted their receivers. "Good morning, Kay. This is Alice."

Kay had to stand tall to speak into the transmitter. "Hi, Alice. I was getting ready to call you."

et al.

"We should go over plans for Christmas dinner."

"Yes, what time would you like to eat?"

"I want to go to church. That ends at twelve. Emmett's church is over then, too. We can be there at 1:00 if that would be okay. We'll bring our presents for your family and your present for Dwain. And could I bring an apple pie?"

"Sounds great, Alice. Is Emmett about ready to go to the Eighty? Jim and Bruce would like to help hay and water the stock cattle this morning."

"He should be there in about an hour."

"Good. He shouldn't try to drive into our driveway. He could get stuck. The boys will meet him on the road."

"Have a good day, Kay."

"Bye, Alice."

Kay hung up along with four others still lingering on the party line. Click, click, click, click.

Jim and Bruce came back from helping Emmett. Sheila had gathered a small pail of eggs. For lunch, they had a cream of tomato soup, chicken salad sandwiches, and chocolate chip cookies. As they finished up, their mother said, "I have a fun job for you. You get to string popcorn and cranberries for the Christmas tree. I have bowls of cranberries and popcorn, and a needle and thread for each of you. Have fun."

Dwain had cut a small cedar tree at the Eighty and fashioned a tree stand from a scrap two-by-four. A white sheet camouflaged the base of this tree. When the first tree he had cut warmed up, its smell had let us know it had been a watering spot for a coyote, and it had to be scrapped in favor of a second tree.

Glass bulbs and homemade paper cutouts left from previous years decorated the newcomer. When in the first grade, Jim had made a five-pointed star covered with fluffed-up cotton, and that hung from the top. Kay had saved from previous Christmases some silvery tinsel; she hung it sparsely from the limbs. Strings of popcorn and cranberries wound round the tree.

"Mom, this is a beautiful tree," said Jim. "Too bad it doesn't have lights."

"You have to have electricity to have lights," Kay said. "Maybe next year."

Jim and Bruce did the chores while it was still light. Then they all waited for Dwain's return.

At 5:30 a 1938 Plymouth pulled into the driveway. Dwain climbed out and grabbed a poor little suitcase with the sticker of Kay's college sorority affixed and entered the back porch. He kissed Kay on the lips. They always kissed when he left and when he returned, even if they had quarreled. Then he hugged each of the children. "Boy, I missed you all," he said.

"Any trouble getting in the driveway" asked Kay.

et al.

"No, the ground is frozen. It's pretty bumpy, though. It's great to be home."

They had a supper of pork neck-bones, vegetables, coleslaw, and canned peaches. After supper Kay cleaned up the dishes and baked a cornbread for the next morning. Everyone got into their pajamas and climbed into the parents' bed. The boys had to sit at the bottom. The family read poetry and played cards and checkers. About 8:00 Kay joined them.

"Well, tomorrow is Christmas Eve," she said. "It's going to be a busy one."

"Want us to help you get ready for Christmas dinner, Kay?"

"Dwain, could you shoot a couple of pheasants? We have a salt-cured pork shoulder, but we could use a little variety in meat. I will have a list of stuff for you boys to fetch from the cave. And Sheila, you can churn the butter and just be Mommy's helper all morning. Tomorrow afternoon I need to pick up the laundry. And we should all take a bath at Alice's in the afternoon. I will wash our sheets and pillowcases there. We will need ice from the stock tank in order to freeze ice cream. I don't care if you wait until Sunday morning if you want."

Dwain said, "Boys, you help your mother after chores for a while. But I will want your help at the Eighty. I'm going to haul some hay. We will need to hitch up the horse to a hay rack."

Soon thereafter, the children were in their own beds. Kay turned the stove down to 2. She made sure the pot of navy beans was in a spot for good heat. Kay and Dwain spooned in bed. "Did your week go okay?" she asked.

"I'm really concerned about our car. It may not last. The damned thing is using a quart of oil every two hundred miles, and it needs all new tires. The four it's got on have over 5000 miles on them and they're almost bald."

As they cuddled, Kay thought, This is more like it. How happy Dwain was going to be when he saw the new suitcase.

December 24

KAY AND DWAIN AWAKENED together. Kay turned up the heat, moved the beans to a spot where they wouldn't burn, and performed her morning duties at the outhouse. All three kids piled into bed with Dwain. They yelled "Happy Christmas Eve" to both parents and each other. One by one the rest of the family made trips out back and settled back into bed while Kay prepared breakfast. The 7:00 whistle blew while father and kids played *Twenty Questions.* "Animal, vegetable, or mineral... It's vegetable and mineral...That's ten questions...No, that shouldn't count... Give up? It's Dad's shotgun."

Cornbread, with lots of butter, and beans was the main course. Dwain had beans for Saturday breakfast in the Navy, and

et al.

he was the main advocate for carrying on the tradition. Coarse-ground meal ground from their own corn made the bread a little crunchy, but it tasted good nonetheless. Homemade applesauce and grape juice rounded out the meal.

Sheila and her mother did the dishes and Bruce and Jim milked Bossy and fed and watered the animals. Kay separated the cream, making sure to reserve plenty for ice cream tomorrow. Kay told the boys, "I want you to bring these things up from the cave; a six-quart kettle of potatoes, six sweet potatoes, two pints of peas, a pint of mulberry jam, a pint of pickled beets, and a couple of tomatoes if you can find any that are still good. Don't bother your father now. He's filling out his weekly report for the VA."

In the late morning Dwain and the boys left with Emmett to take care of the cattle at the Eighty. When they returned, lunch was on the table; leftover beans and cornbread, macaroni and cheese, and coleslaw containing one of their last good tomatoes.

After lunch Dwain said, "Kay, I left something for you on the back porch. Two rooster pheasants."

"Oh, thanks. I'll dress them right away." She went out to the burn barrel, cleaned the birds, threw the guts and feathers on top of crinkled up newspapers, and lit a fire. She cut the birds in pieces and left them to soak in salt water. She hoped she had cut out all of the lead shot.

After lunch Kay went to the phone and cranked longer than long. "Operator," said Ruth Boles.

"Please connect me with the Emmett Daughton residence," said Kay.

"Here you are," said Ruth.

"Hello," said Alice.

"Is it okay to come over now?" asked Kay.

"Absolutely. See you when you get here."

Kay hung up to a chorus of party line clicks.

All five Daughtons loaded into the car along with one basket of dirty clothes, another basket of sheets and pillowcases, a gallon bucket of cream, and an empty ten-gallon cream can for water. The first stop was to let the kids off at their grandparents' house for baths. The next stop was to exchange the dirty clothes at Goldey's for a basket of clean clothes. Kay didn't like having another woman do their washing, but what could she do? No running water, no electricity. But it was nice to have the clothes ironed and folded. Still, three dollars. That was a lot. The third stop was at Vera Brown's store. She weighed the cream and measured its butterfat content and gave Kay $2.22.

At Alice's, the kids had finished their baths. Kay washed the week's bedding and put them in a basket, and it was Kay's turn for a bath. She luxuriated in a half-full tub of hot water. She always looked forward to this, as trying to stay clean with a small basin of water during the week was almost impossible. Dwain decided against a bath as he had taken a shower the previous morning at the hotel in Council Bluffs. He filled the water can.

On the way home, they stopped at Pinky Green's Grocery. The kids and Dwain bought five-cent ice cream cones. Kay bought two loaves of sliced bread and a head of lettuce for Christmas dinner, and hot dog buns, a package of wieners, and a can of chili for a quick supper.

It was mid-afternoon by the time they returned home. Using clothespins, Kay hung the sheets and pillowcases on the line. They quickly froze as stiff as boards, but with a light breeze, Kay knew they would be dry in a few hours.

After supper Dwain and the kids got ready to go to town. The kids saw a Tom Mix movie in a deserted building, and Dwain enjoyed playing pitch in the smoky back room of the filling station. They played for money, but rarely a loss or a profit exceeded two dollars. Dwain was a good player, most often a winner.

Kay stayed home. First, she put away the week's clean clothes. The sheets from the clothesline were dry and smelled wonderful, and she made the beds. Then she did prep work for the Christmas dinner. She diced the lettuce and prepared a dressing for the salad. She peeled and diced the potatoes, and peeled the sweet potatoes as well, leaving both kinds of potatoes soaking in water.

She turned on the battery radio. *Your Hit Parade* was already playing. She loved listening to the top twenty. Her favorite performer was Hoagie Carmichael. Kay was pulling for *Buttermilk Skies* to finish number one this week.

It was time to get out the presents for the kids. Each of the boys got a pair of blue jeans and a shirt she had made from feed sacks. Sheila got a homemade blue velvet jumper and a skirt made of feed sacks. Sheila and Kay got a kick from picking out the sacks for her dress, but the boys didn't care which sacks she used. Kay's treadle sewing machine worked well, but she could have wished for better light than the gas lamp.

She wrapped the presents and hid them in her wardrobe, and then mused about a perfect present for her husband. Dwain was handsome, and yes, a little vain. When he left for work his suit had to be neatly pressed and his shirt and tie just so. He was close-shaven, and his thinning hair was brushed neat, like Beau Brummell's. She could image him showing up at a hotel with her old suitcase with the Hillsdale College gummed sticker. He would probably try to hide it by keeping his body between the clerk and the old, tattered thing. She could imagine how his face will light up tomorrow when he sees his new brown leather luggage.

She heard cars doors slam and the rest of the family came in from the porch. The laughed and joked with one another as they got ready for bed. Kay turned down the oil furnace. When the children were asleep, she got stockings from her wardrobe. All three kids got an orange and a Baby Ruth candy bar. Sheila got a game of jacks, Bruce got a baseball, and Jim the card game Authors. She put their wrapped presents under the tree and turned off the lamp.

As she climbed into bed next to Dwain, she said," Well, I guess we're ready for Christmas."

"Yes, thanks to you, Dear."

"How did you do in pitch?"

"I won a little more than two dollars."

"Good night, Darling."

December 25

THERE WAS NO 7:00AM whistle on Sunday, but that wasn't needed that morning. All three kids piled into their parents' bed crying, "Merry Christmas, Merry Christmas." They were excited about getting presents, even if they had pretty good guesses what they were.

Kay arose and turned up the furnace and lit the lamp. She was first in the parade to the outhouse, and then set the teakettle on the stove so everyone could wash his/her hands with hot water. She turned the radio to a station dedicated to Christmas music, and then announced they could go to the living room and look in their stockings and open their presents.

The openings were completed in a matter of minutes. Both Sheila and Bruce gave Jim a tube of BBs for his gun. Jim gave Sheila a Bambi comb and Bruce a slingshot. Bruce gave Sheila a coloring book that also could be used as paper dolls. Sheila gave Bruce a toy gun. The three children made Christmas cards for each parent, each contributing a small Crayola drawing. The children took turns thanking their parents and each other for presents, and they gave special thanks to the mother for her hand-made items.

Dwain went to their bedroom and came back with a bottle of Jergens hand cream and gave it to Kay.

"Alice said this was the best," he said.

Kay's hands were red and chapped, and she often tried to hide them. "Thanks, Dear. I really needed this. Your present will be delivered when your folks come over this afternoon."

The boys went out to do chores and their father went along to inspect. Afterwards, he said, "I think you boys are finally doing things right."

They came back to a breakfast of fried sidemeat and scrambled eggs with toast. As a special treat each got a very small glass of freshly squeezed orange juice.

et al.

After breakfast, Dwain and Sheila drove to the Eighty and Bruce and Jim dressed for church. They wore their new blue jeans and the shirts their mother had made. They pulled on their four-buckle overshoes and walked the mile to church getting there well before the second bell. In the meantime, Kay prepared dinner at home.

She removed a salt-cured pork shoulder from the icebox. The fresh meat had been a present from Dwain's brother Jim, who had butchered. Kay had coated and rubbed the pork with smoke-flavored salt and had left it to age in a four-gallon stone crock for three weeks. After removal, the salt was brushed off before storage in the icebox. That morning, Kay washed the shoulder, placed it in a roaster pan, and put it in the oven at medium heat.

She peeled and cut up white potatoes into sugar-cube size and boiled them until just tender. In a separate pan she made a white sauce of milk, cream, butter, and cornstarch, added the potatoes and two pints of her canned peas. She added pepper and salt to taste.

The sweet potatoes were sliced and laid in a baking dish and covered with pats of butter and drizzled with pancake syrup. The dish was placed alongside the pork in the oven.

She mixed chopped lettuce with a dressing and set it in a large dish on the table on the porch, where it was just above freezing.

Cream, milk, sugar, vanilla, and a custard mix were poured into the freezer can for making ice cream. Sheila and Dwain were to bring back ice from the Eighty and crush it in a burlap bag by striking the bag with the flat side of a two-bladed ax.

Kay set the dining room table for seven. Dwain and Emmett were to sit at the ends, Alice and Kay were to sit on one side, and the three children on the other. She used her mother's china and silver-plated knives, forks, and spoons laid on a white, lace tablecloth for the adults. The children's place settings were a hodgepodge of survivors from past residences and garage sales.

Sheila and Dwain arrived home with a burlap bag with fifteen pounds of ice, which they broke up. They placed the can containing liquid in the freezer, added crushed ice, and lots of coarse salt, and started cranking. In about fifteen minutes they could no longer turn the crank—the ice cream was frozen.

Kay removed all traces of cigarette butts and ashes before their company arrived. Alice was didn't approve of her smoking, any woman's smoking for that matter. But Kay knew Alice knew she smoked.

Emmett drove up the driveway with the car swaying to and fro over the bumps but was able to park next to the Plymouth. Alice, a little shaken, got out and came inside with her husband.

Alice said, "Oh, Kathryn what a beautiful table! You've outdone yourself."

et al.

"Thank you," said Kay. I'm glad you like it. You know, I think we should have our gift exchange before dinner, don't you?"

"That's a good idea," said Alice.

They gathered in the living room. Kay's family gave Alice her favorite perfume, Evening in Paris, and Emmett a box of Prince Albert cigars. Dwain got fencing pliers and Kay a set of linen handkerchiefs from Alice and Emmett, Alice gave Sheila a white cotton blouse to go with the skirt Kay had made.

The boys got special gifts, nylon shirts. Throughout the war, parachutes took all available nylon. Alice had gone to Des Moines and bought some of the very first nylon shirts available. "Thank you very much, Alice," said Jim,

"Me too," said Bruce.

Alice beamed.

"I guess it's time for my gift to Dwain," said Kay. "Jim, could you go to their car and bring it in?"

Jim returned with a large bundle wrapped in white tissue. Dwain removed the paper to reveal a brown cowhide beauty, about three feet tall, still faintly smelling of the tanning process. Kay watched her husband's face, fully expecting him to break out in joy. "Kay, we can't afford expensive things like this!" Kay was crushed.

Alice said, "You shush, Dwain. She saved all her egg money to buy that for you."

"Mom, we are really pinched right now. But I suppose I really could use a better suitcase."

They sat down to a sumptuous meal. As usual, Emmett put too much horseradish on his meat, and although his face turned crimson, he managed to eat it all. Kay was disappointed the pork didn't taste smokier. She had wanted it to be like a smoked ham. Ice cream and Alice's apple pie finished a wonderful Christmas dinner.

Alice said, "Dwain, set up the pitch game. Kay and I will clean up the dishes."

Dwain said, "First, you boys take all this wrapping paper to the barrel and burn it before we play cards."

Dwain got out a card table, five chairs, a deck of cards, and a paper and pencil to keep score. The boys set a roaring fire in the burn barrel and came back inside to play pitch.

"Hey, everyone, I can't find my shirt," said Bruce. "Do one of you have it with your stuff?"

Panic set in. The shirt was nowhere to be found. The possibility that it was burned with the wrapping paper loomed. Dwain dashed from the house and tipped over the barrel. Ashes and cans were still hot. He took a garden rake spread the contents on the ground. They told the awful truth. Oyster-shell buttons.

et al.

Dwain raged. "God Damn it, Bruce. How could you burn up that shirt? And I hold you responsible, too, Jim."

"Oh Dwain, it's a shame," said Alice. "But I'll buy another."

"Like hell you will. He will do without. I can only hope it teaches him a lesson."

Bruce fought back tears.

The two women went back to work in the kitchen, Kay washing, Alice drying.

"I wanted a joyful Christmas, but things seem to have gone really wrong," said Kay.

"Oh, the shirt burned, and Dwain was upset about the cost of that beautiful suitcase. Neither of those things amount to a hill of beans. My mother died when I was eight, never saw me grow up, get married, and have her grandchildren. My little Dwight died in my arms when he was two years old. Just couldn't save him. Life goes on. You just have to take the bitter with the sweet. I'll bet when you are as old as I am now, you'll look at these times as the best of your life."

"You may be right, Alice, but right now I'm disappointed. I wanted to make this Christmas special. We've had some hard times since the war ended, and I thought we had made enough progress to celebrate. Dwain is still fixated about money."

"You're getting a late start in saving for your kids' college and your own retirement. Dwain is thirty-six years old. He isn't going to change anytime soon."

"You are probably right, Alice. And thanks for the advice."

They took off their aprons and sat in the living room to watch the others play cards. The participants laughed, moaned and groaned, and argued about rules.

About 4:00PM, Alice and Emmett left for their car. Alice said, "What a wonderful Christmas. Thank you so much."

Bruce and Jim made quick work of their chores. There were plenty of leftovers for supper. After the dishes were cleared, everyone put on pajamas, and climbed into bed, preparing to listen to the Sunday night radio shows: Amos and Andy, Fiber Magee and Mollie, George and Gracie Allen, Edgar Bergen and Charlie McCarthy, and Jack Benny. Bruce and Jim played checkers at the foot of the bed. Sheila lay between her mother and her father and had to fight off sleep.

Kay absorbed the peaceful scene and considered Alice's advice. *Maybe this really is the best time of my life.*

Hiring Out

"BIG DAY FOR YOU tomorrow, huh Jim?" Bobby's whisper floated to the top bunk. Their mother had just turned off the gas lamp. Moonlight flooded into their bedroom, which was just large enough to hold their bunk and a wardrobe, and still leave a little shuffling room to enter and leave.

"Yeah. My first job for hire."

"And if they pay you, you can keep the money?"

"Yep. Not like when we work here on our farm. We sweat and pull our guts out and always get a kick in the butt or a leather strap across our legs for not trying hard enough or for not being careful enough."

"And Dad keeps calling us *shithooks*. What's a *shithook*, anyway?"

"I don't know, Little Brother. It's just some lingo he picked up in the Navy in WWII. I don't think it's a compliment."

et al.

"Dad will be on travel until Friday, so there will be some peace around here until then. Good night, Jim."

"Good night, Bobby."

AT SUNUP THE BOYS rolled out of bed, dressed, and attended to chores. Bobby milked two cows in the little barn. With light streaming through dusty windows no kerosene lamp was needed. Jim fed and watered twenty pigs, one hundred chickens, and pumped water into the stock tank. The latter chore was much easier now with the installation of a pump powered by a converted Model T engine. All you had to do was crank a heavy flywheel fast and choke the gas until spark ignition, and lo and behold the engine went "putt putt putt" and the pump drew water up from sixty feet below and poured a stream through a pipe and into the stock tank. It only took five minutes to pump enough water for the whole day. Before the engine Jim needed his whole weight to pull the pump handle down, and it was all he could do to finish in thirty minutes.

Their mother had fired up the propane stove to prepare a breakfast of scrambled eggs and bacon along with buttered bread and jelly glasses full of last year's tomato juice, which could be kept cool on the icebox so long as the ice block wasn't melted. The boys chowed down.

Jim made a trip to the water bucket and drank from the ladle. He didn't want to start off the day thirsty. "Got to get going, Mom. Johnny Fields wants me at his place at seven."

"Have you finished all of your work assignments? Your father said you couldn't work for someone else until you had finished your work here. You know how he is if he thinks he's been disobeyed."

"Yes, Mom. Yesterday Bobby and I weeded the garden, picked and shelled the peas, and hoed thistles in the pasture. Everything was done."

"Be sure to wear a long sleeved shirt, straw hat, and leather gloves."

"I will, Mom. I should be home a little after six."

Jim climbed on his bike and pedaled over a dirt road two miles to the Fields farm leaving a dust trail behind. It was already hot, and the day promised to be a scorcher. He deployed the kickstand by a tree in the back yard of Fields's small, white farmhouse and knocked at the door. Johnny answered, "Be right with you. Niles is on his way."

The seven o'clock whistle could be heard from Grand River, three miles away.

Niles Gibbs drove his orange Allis Chalmers tractor pulling a hayrack into the farmyard. "You feeling strong today, Jim? We got some hay to put up."

et al.

"You bet, Niles. I'm ready to go."

Johnny joined them and said, "There's about 500 round bales ready waiting across the road. They're calling for rain tomorrow, so let's get to it." He climbed on a small, red Farmall tractor and drove into the field pulling a second empty hayrack. The hay bales were scattered across the field where the baler had kicked them out. Johnny left his tractor parked and joined Niles and Jim at the "Little Alice."

The two older men owned adjacent farms and traded work. Niles was seventy and had heart problems. He wore Key overalls, a long sleeved blue chambray cotton shirt, and a straw hat with an oily sweatband. He rolled his own and was in the process of smoking one.

Johnny was sixty-five and limped from a horse riding accident. He had blue jeans and a leather belt with a large silver buckle. He wore a cowboy shirt and a leather hat, also with a sweatband that had seen lots of action. Johnny was chewing Red Man. "We can load about sixty-four bales on each rack and then put them in the haymow. Niles can drive the tractor and I can stack the load. Do you think you can throw bales on the rack, Jim?"

"I'm almost fifteen and I'll be a sophomore in high school this fall. I'm five foot ten and weigh a hundred and thirty pounds. I'm pretty strong."

"Good," said Johnny. "Let's get started. Some of the hay in that low spot over there had some weeds, and the bales will weigh eighty pounds or more. So let's load them first for the bottom rows. We don't want to lift the heavy ones any higher than we have to."

Niles drove with Johnny standing on the rack. Jim walked alongside and threw the bales on the rack as he came to them. Both Johnny and Jim wielded hay hooks in their right hands, tools with wooden handles and hooks with very sharp tips. Jim would use the hook to pull the bale on end with the top of the bale near his belt buckle. Then he would bend forward slightly over the bale and hook its bottom. He would pull the bottom of the bale up hard past horizontal and using his knee would continue the upward motion of the bale. For higher lifts, his arms could raise the bale so its upper end could reach nine feet. The person on the rack could then use his hay hook to pull the bale aboard. Until today Jim had done very little of this kind of work, but he caught on quickly. Johnny took the bales and stacked an orderly load with four layers, each with sixteen bales.

Bales in the low spot were indeed very heavy, and it was all Jim could do to pitch them on the hayrack. Thistles bristled from the bales, and he was glad for long sleeves and jeans that gave him partial protection, but in a short time his arms and legs bore scratches that smarted from sweat. Blisters started to form on his hands from grasping the hay hook despite his leather gloves.

"You gonna feed these bales to your cattle, Johnny? There's lotsa weeds in 'em."

et al.

"It's true the hay is poor, Niles, but this winter it'll beat a snow bank all to hell as far as the cattle are concerned." Both older men chuckled.

This labor continued until both racks were loaded full. They drove them to Johnny's big red barn. Niles parked his hayrack under the hayloft door, unhitched his tractor, and drove it to the other end of the barn. There a rope hung down and Niles attached it to his tractor's hitch. "Ready to go, Johnny," he yelled.

Over Johnny's wagon a hay hook hung from a rope. In principle the hook worked like ice tongs, only there were four tongs instead of two. A load of six bales could be secured in its grasp. This rope was attached at the other end to Niles's tractor by passing through pulleys near the roof at each end of the barn and along a trolley running along the underside of the roof. Given the okay signal, Niles would pull the load up into the barn. Once inside the haymow, the six bales could be released by pulling on a trip rope that traveled along with the load. The timing of release would determine where in the mow the bales would be dropped.

Jim's job was to pull the dropped bales to the edges of the mow and arrange them in some order. The physical task was not so difficult, but the environment was dusty and hot, dusty from bouncing bales and much hotter than outside because the hay was still curing. Johnny had given Jim a bucket of salt to sprinkle on the greenest bales.

The fun part of the job for Jim was to yell "OK drop it" when the load was positioned at a good spot in the mow. It was exciting to watch the bales bounce in random directions.

After both loads were stowed away, Johnny said, "Let's take a break." Niles rolled a cigarette and Johnny grabbed some Red Man for himself after offering Jim some. Jim had politely refused.

Then they passed around the water jug, a glass gallon bottle wrapped in wet burlap. Niles and Johnny both drank and passed the jug to Jim. Johnny had brown liquid left over from the Red Man at the corners of his mouth, which gave some reason for Jim to hesitate, but he was so thirsty he drank deeply.

"Well, we'd best get back at it," said Johnny.

They picked up the third and fourth loads of the day and stored them in the barn. While loading the top bales of the last load, Jim felt a little dizzy, but willed himself to keep going. He recovered when he got a little rest on the ride to the barn. Jim had hay fever, and the dusty haymow set off sneezing episodes. His only handkerchief was wringing wet from snot and his shirt was soaked with sweat. Dust and hay particles clung to his face, hair, and arms. As the last of the bales were mowed back, the noon whistle sounded in Grand River.

"Well, that's 256 bales that won't get wet tomorrow," said Johnny. "Let's see what Ruth and Ellen cooked for lunch."

et al.

A table with five chairs sat in a shady spot in the back yard. Two ladies both wearing print dresses and aprons met them. Ruth Fields said, "You boys are too dirty to come in the house, so we'll eat out here. You can get some of the worst off over by the pump. There are washcloths and towels for you there."

How wonderful it felt to wash in that cool water. "I feel almost human again," Jim said as walked to the table where the others sat.

Ellen Gibbs looked Jim up and down. "Looks like you could use some good food. You're skinny as a rail."

"Well, I'm ready to eat," Jim said. "I'm really hungry."

Piled on the table was a hearty meal. The women had killed two chickens and had fried them golden brown, country style. Butter floated on top of a bowl of mashed potatoes, and cream gravy was ready to top them. Ruth had sacrificed one of her quart jars of canned beef to mix with long, homemade noodles. A bowl of fresh, shelled green peas sat next to a plate of hot buttermilk biscuits. Two pitchers sat in the middle of the table, one filled with tea and the other with lemonade.

Jim couldn't believe he could eat so much. He had seconds of everything. And when he didn't think he could eat any more, Ruth said, "Now it's time for pie."

She went to the house and returned with a lemon chiffon pie, the chiffon rising four inches above the tangy lemon pudding. Jim ate a big piece of that, too. "I think this was the best meal I ever had," said Jim.

After the other two men also gave the women accolades for the food, they rested in the shade. Jim lay nearby, flat on the grass, and could have gone to sleep if he hadn't been so uncomfortable after such a big meal. Earlier than Jim would have liked, Johnny said, "Well I guess we should get back to it."

Although slightly unsteady when he stood up, Jim recovered and worked the rest of the day without missing a beat. It got very hot, and he was even sweatier and dirtier and snottier than after the mornings work.

With the last bale stowed, Johnny said, "Well, we got 'er done. I guess it's time to settle up." They sat in the shade and had a drink of water. The six o'clock siren sounded in Grand River.

"What do you think we owe him, Niles?"

"Well, I hear these days hired hands get five dollars for a day's work. I think Jim here has done everything today we could have expected, and I reckon he should get paid accordingly."

"I agree," said Johnny. "You did a good job, Jim." Johnny dug a leather coin purse from his jeans. From it he took out a roll of bills, peeled off five one-dollar bills, and handed them to Jim. "Thanks, Jim."

"Thank *you* very much," said Jim.

et al.

"Do you think you could help us again this summer?" asked Niles.

"Oh sure, any time so long as I'm not needed on our farm," said Jim.

Johnny said, "We'll be a calling ya."

Jim climbed on his bike and headed home.

"Nice kid," said Johnny.

"Yeah," said Niles. "And I hear his Dad treats him pretty rough. Maybe working for us might make Jim feel better."

"Agreed," said Johnny.

Jim was elated. He wanted to pedal faster, but the muscles in the backs of his legs started to cramp, so he traveled at a slower pace. The blisters on his hand had broken, so he didn't grab the bicycle handles too firmly. When his bike was parked in the yard, he went to the back door and met his mother standing there. She took one look at him and said, "Don't you even *think* about coming in this house. Here is a washcloth and a towel. When you have done your chores, go down the stock tank and wash off the outer layer. You can do the final cleanup on the back porch."

Jim fed the livestock and dropped by the barn. Bobby was just bringing out two buckets of milk. "How did it go, Brother?"

"Just great. I'll tell you more later."

The stock tank was still full enough from this morning, so no pumping was needed. Jim took off his clothes and climbed in. He pushed some green algae aside so could sit in the tank. *This feels good*, he thought. *I hope the cows won't mind how my dirty body is flavoring the water.*

He dried off, put his clean clothes on, and headed to the house where his mother had spaghetti with tomato sauce, a fresh salad from their garden—lettuce, green onions, and radishes...and strawberry shortcake for dessert. While they were eating, they listened to the news. That was a treat. They had to ration the expensive radio battery.

"Jim, did you get paid?" his mother asked.

"Yes, Mom. I got five dollars."

"Put it in your college jar. It will all add up."

"Yes, Mom. I already did it."

IN BED THAT NIGHT after the lights were out, Bobby asked, "What's it like, hiring out? Did the money make you feel good?"

"Yep. I liked the money. Do you know what else I liked, maybe even more. They said I did a good job. And they thanked me."

Fire Call

"*B*ILLY, DO YOU READ ME?" squawked a voice from the portable Motorola radio.

"Ten Four, Harry. What's up?"

"Need you to load your guys on the truck and get your butts to headquarters ASAP. You boys are going to a fire."

In mid-July 1955, supper at the mess tent was just ending after a workday at a remote camp in the Coeur d'Alene National Forest. Blister rust control (BRC) in white pine plantations was our regular job but fighting forest fires took priority for all Forest Service employees. Our BRC crew had been placed on fire watch and was prepared for the call. Twenty-three of us pivoted off the benches, walked quickly to our own four-man tents to grab our tools, hard hats, gloves, a change of clothes, and WWI Army canteens, and climbed in the truck bed with Billy, the camp boss, at the wheel.

Since the fire season had begun with summer thunderstorms, I had been looking forward the extra income

et al.

from fires to help me through my junior year of engineering at Iowa State University. Our regular workweek was forty-eight hours (only forty if it rained) at $2.00 per hour, and the forest service deducted $1.95 a day for meals from our paychecks. I would work more than twice my normal hours on fires and the meals were free. The extra money determined whether I could pay for my next year in college.

Trail Creek camp was forty-two miles over narrow and winding dirt roads from Coeur d'Alene, Idaho, but Billy Gibbs drove the distance in less than an hour, the rear wheels of the two-and-a-half-ton Ford truck throwing up dust and sliding around curves overlooking precipitous drop-offs. We sat in two rows facing the middle of the truck bed.

"Oh shit," yelled one passenger, "Billy's gonna kill us before the fire gets its turn at us."

"What the fuck you worried about, asshole? Billy's got a chauffeur's license," said one of Billy's friends.

At the main ranger station, we were greeted by Harry Faulkner, the forest supervisor. He was dark and wiry, an ex-logger with a pockmarked face and a gravelly voice that sounded like there were iron gears in his voice box that had never been oiled. A long-retired Greyhound bus was parked next to the headquarters building. "This here vehicle is taking you to Darby, Montana. The fire is in the Bitterroot drainage. You'll get further instructions when you get there. You've got your tools, hard hats, and canteens?"

"Yep, we do," said Billy.

"Good luck then. See ya when you get back."

"Thanks," drawled Billy. He was slim and well-tanned with slicked-down black hair. He had worked three summers in the forest between school years at Northern Alabama University, and the coming year he would be starting law school. His good looks and self-assurance inspired trust in both forest supervisors and our crew of twenty-three, all white college students. We boarded a bus for the long ride to Darby, Montana, about 250 miles distant.

The young passengers prided themselves in swearing and tobacco usage. Four or five profanities might pop up in a single sentence, about half the swear words contained some form of the F-bomb. Nervous laughter disguised worries about forest fire dangers. Some boys smoked cigars or cigarettes while chewing tobacco at the same time. There were dirty jokes and singing. One song was:

et al.

> "We're Uncle Billy's raiders, we're riders of the night.
>
> We're dirty son-a-bitches, we'd rather fuck than fight.
>
> Highty Dighty, Christ Almighty, Who in the hell are we?
>
> Rim Ram, God Damn, BRC."

In spite of the apparently jovial and carefree mood, there was an undercurrent of fear. Just six years before, thirteen firefighters had died, twelve of them smoke jumpers, in the Mann Gulch forest fire near Helena, Montana. Our crew had trained for firefighting on a couple of rainy days, and instructors had emphasized safety. We had some faith in the forest service, but all the same, based on history, we couldn't really trust them completely.

On the bus, I sat next to Max Raeder. He was older than the rest, a Korean War veteran, a junior in Forestry at Oregon State, small and wiry, and he sported an unkempt beard. He had been a squad leader in the war but refused to talk about his experiences. He'd turned down chances be a camp boss, had said he never wanted to run anything again. Unlike the rest of us, he had several years of forest fire experience. He nearly always wore a smile and seemed easily amused.

"Max, is this going to be dangerous?" I asked.

"It shouldn't be. The biggest risk you probably face is cutting yourself with your ax," Max said.

"Max, you ever been on a fire where someone died?"

"Yeah once. On a Salmon River fire, a guy got bonked on the head by a falling tree. It was a strange accident. The fire burned at the base of the tree, and the wind kept it upright. Toward evening, the wind calmed down, and the tree fell silently. Split the poor fucker's hardhat. They cleared a landing pad for a helicopter to take him to the hospital, but he was DOA."

"I know there could be accidents like that, but what if the fire races toward you like it did at Mann Gulch? What should you do?"

"A fire can travel sixty miles per hour. You probably should sit, put your head between your legs, and kiss your ass goodbye."

"I'm really not worried. Just thought I'd ask."

"There's a good thing about going out that way, though."

"What's that, Max?"

"Saves a lot on cremation fees."

We rode in silence as the bus rolled east on US 10 through the panhandle of Idaho, through Kellogg and Wallace, and then across the divide into Montana. Twilight turned to night as the bus went south from Missoula, home of the smoke jumpers, toward Darby. At 11:00 PM we turned off the highway and onto a dirt road to a waiting cattle truck.

"Everyone off the bus and onto the truck," said the bus driver.

et al.

"Alright, let's do it," barked Billy.

We had to stand in the truck's bed as it had no seats. One of our crew cried out, "God Damn! What's this? There's cow shit on my hand. They could have cleaned this fucker up a little before we got on." Everyone tried to find a clean handhold rack as the truck bounced along a primitive road that would have been impassable for the bus. A forest service ranger met us at the trailhead and issued every second man a head lamp. "You've got a little walk ahead of you. These lights will help you see the trail."

The *little walk* was six miles at night along Tin Cup Creek, a fast, clear, and ice-cold stream about ten feet wide. We were off in single file along a narrow foot trail. A half-moon shined through scattered clouds to aid the headlamps in identifying obstacles in and along the trail. The trail was sometimes steep up, sometimes steep down, sometimes level. It ran along the left of the creek, crossed over a crude log bridge, and then followed the creek on the right. Then it returned back across another bridge to the left. Waterfalls and cataracts made a deafening roar near the stream but dimmed as the trail left the creek. We walked through the night as though in a trance, almost like sleep walking, careful not to fall while carrying sharp tools. We walked about four hours, taking ten minutes to rest every hour. Most smoked on the break, including me. Many others just fell asleep.

We saw a dull orange glow on the horizon ahead. It wasn't the sun—we were headed generally west. No, it was the fire. The glow expanded as we neared, and it inspired awe, much as battle sounds must affect soldiers coming into battle. As we got nearer, we could see the fire spreading out on the north side of Tin Cup Creek. Light from the fire revealed large, black areas where the fire had eaten all fuel, and flames dancing along the ground around its periphery. Smoke billowed overhead, and even near the burned-out areas, the smell from smoldering coals was powerful. The fire covered an area of a little over 1000 acres, about two sections.

Packhorses had hauled in some equipment and supplies for a primitive fire camp. A snorting pole made from a freshly cut small pine was nailed between two bigger pines, with a slit trench dug below it. Even some toilet paper was furnished, but inevitably, pine pitch stuck on your butt if you used the pole. After one experience on the pole, most of us opted for pooping in the woods like bears. Each of us received a bag with oranges, sandwiches, and two cans of beans for our breakfast and lunch. We threw our sacks of spare clothes in a pile, and as the sun was coming up, we went directly to the fire line without sleep.

Fire crews built a narrow, fuel-free line around the fire to contain it. Ours was a typical crew: four axmen (I was one) blazed the trail and cut small trees four feet on either side of the prospective line with double-bladed axes. Next came eight men with Pulaskis, named for a famous forest fighter, Edward Crockett Pulaski. The tool was both a single-bladed ax and a grubbing tool used to cut and root out bushes and small trees, which were then cast away from the fire side of a three-foot-wide line cut into soil. Six men with shovels followed, digging out smaller roots and digging into the dirt along the line. They were followed by two sawyers who sawed out sections of logs lying across the fire line. In those days before chain saws were used on fires, four-foot long crosscut saws were manned by men at either end. A cleanup shovel man completed the line, ridding the trail of sawdust and dirt that had been under the log. The last person on the crew was the waterbuck, who carried a large canvas bag with water gathered from the nearest flowing water. The waterbuck was highly valued on a hot day. A crew boss called breaks and looked out for the crew's safety from hazards such as wind changes or falling trees. A good crew could build a trail at about the speed of a very leisurely walk. The trail was cut around the fire, just over the ridge top from where it was burning.

At midmorning, we heard a loud explosion. "What the hell was that?" I asked.

Max Raeder said, "That was the fire crowning. The heat from ground fire dried out the treetops, and with lower humidity this morning, the fire exploded to the treetops all the way to the ridge top."

Billie said, "We're not going to be uphill or downwind from the fire. We won't let that son-of-a-bitch hurt you guys."

Fire trails of the kind we built couldn't stop a crowning fire. You just got out of the way and prayed for rain. But once a line is built around the fire, a mop-up procedure could start, working from the fire line in toward the center, piling dirt on anything burning to put out remaining hot spots.

We were really hungry on our first day on the fire line, but were sorely disappointed with our bags of food. The lunchmeats in the sandwiches were of two kinds. The larger diameter we called *horse cock*, the smaller diameter, *donkey dick*. Both were dry like paper and tasteless. The bitter oranges were the size of large walnuts. Luckily, we could open the bean cans with an ax, but the beans, too, were of poor quality. We ate them with pairs of pealed sticks. Some guys heaved unopened cans into the fire and waited for the inevitable explosion.

Every hour, Billy called a rest break with "Take five." We would rest for ten minutes, about half of us falling to sleep. Then he would yell, "Let's get back to it." We had to gently shake some sleepyheads.

We worked until after dark and staggered back to the fire camp, which had been only slightly improved. Famished, but too tired to care much about eating, we each got a plate of stew and a sleeping bag, and then found an empty spot on the ground. I happened to pick a very large, flat rock, which was naturally quite hard, but that wasn't the biggest problem. My bag was short for my six-foot one-inch frame and it got really cold. I curled up to get my shoulders covered, but as I dozed off, I straightened, and the bag and I caterpillared down the slope of my rock. This repeated until 4:30 AM when I was ten feet down the mountain from where I'd started.

et al.

"Take your hands off your cocks and onto your socks. It's daylight in the swamp," came a booming voice from the camp. I could have slugged the guy who woke us up, but I shrugged and rolled up my sleeping bag. I shivered from the cold as I reached for my hard hat, which was coated with frost. After a cup of coffee and a couple of rolls, our crew once again got bags of food for lunch and went back on the fire line.

As darkness approached that evening, we returned to a fire camp that had been transformed. A galley was set , and we had a fabulous supper of steak, potatoes, salad, cake, and lemonade. I took my distended stomach along with a longer sleeping bag and found a soft and level bedding area. I slept like a baby and was more ready to take on another sixteen-hour day the following morning.

After a week of this schedule, we were a sorry sight. Each of us had brought a shirt and one spare pair of socks and underwear. On day three of the fire we put on the spares. The shirt I had been wearing was stiff from perspiration salt, and the clean shirt felt good. Then came the mop-up phase of firefighting. We waded through ashes to mix dirt with glowing coals where tree stumps had once been. On day six of the fire, my new shirt was so dirty that I put on my original. A few bars of soap were made available by an ice-cold mountain creek, and I washed my hands and face, but the rest of my body remained grime-coated.

At last we were told the fire was contained and we could go home. We traveled back to our home base, all very smoky, stinky, dirty, and tired. We walked down to the trailhead, took a truck back to the highway and a bus back to Coeur d'Alene. The bus ride was quiet. There were no rowdy jokes, no singing, lots of sleeping. Only the driver stayed awake. From the ranger station Billy drove our truck back to camp. A shower and clean clothes never felt so good!

I had initially feared a forest fire. I knew it could be dangerous. But I got 110 hours of pay that week, the first 36 hours without sleep, and I could pay my way through college the next year. And none of us really got hurt, just a few cuts and bruises. One more fire and maybe I could buy a car.

At supper, I sat next to Max. "Want to go on another fire?" he asked.

"Bring it on," I said.

Hotspot

To: Friends and Family
Date: January 5, 2012
Subject: Hotspot

As I lamented in my last email, our vacation condo on Coronado Island didn't have Wi-Fi. Well, Della and I had to find some way to satisfy our internet addiction. The attendant in the lobby said we could use our iPhone to connect the internet to our Mac, so after lunch we targeted an Apple Store, planning to use MapQuest to get there in our rental car.

The early instructions read, *turn left in 50 feet, then right on Seaside Avenue for 120 feet, then...* We didn't pay much attention to those because we knew where Interstate 5 was anyway, and so we just drove there. The middle instructions were important, though, because we had to *go three miles to 163 and then go another 3.2 miles to the California Freeway,* and there were plenty of wrong exits we could have taken which may have led to places from which we could never return.

et al.

Two somewhat visually impaired and severely hard-of-hearing old people did manage to enter the busy freeway system. I drove, and Della was co-pilot with a Hertz San Diego map on her lap. I managed to enter correct lanes with a lot of "Better get over one lane." and "Oops, that's exit only," and "Not this turn or the next, but the one after that," and we managed to get close enough to see the shopping center we sought. The last several MapQuest instructions were about as confusing and useless as the first few. With all three final turns in less than the length of a football field, we didn't need them. We could even see Bloomingdales and knew the Apple store was nearby. We parked in the ramp, entered the maze, and saw the Apple Store right before us. We thought our internet connection problem was practically solved. But it wasn't even the end of the beginning.

The store had varnished-cement floors and a high ceiling, perfect for reflecting and re-reflecting sound. People were packed inside with standing room only and talking incessantly; it was hard to hear yourself think. After a few minutes of hanging around and looking lost, we were approached by a good-looking black man who said, "You are number nine on my list. I will get someone to help you in about ten to fifteen minutes."

We stood nearby, and after a while Della wondered, "How does he remember our position in the waiting list? He didn't write anything down." So, she asked him, and he tapped his temple to indicate the information was stored inside.

A little later, a cute blonde girl asked if she could help. We explained our problem, and she took down the serial number of our iPhone. After punching keys on a little hand-held computer, she gave us some bad news. "Although your iPhone is less than two years old, it is too old to support a hotspot." She offered to get us a technician to help us, and we agreed.

Russ, a salesman disguised as technical support, introduced himself. "Hi, I'm Rusty."

"I'm a little rusty myself," I said.

"You've got a comic for a husband, I see," Russ said with an annoyed chuckle.

"He says stuff like that all the time," Della said patiently.

Rusty verified that our phone, while still a perfectly good one, would not handle a hotspot. But there was some really good news. If we qualified (he said this seriously), we could get a great upgrade deal. For only $100 and signing a new contract, we could get an iPhone that would work for a hotspot. For $200 and signing a new contract, we could get an iPhone with still more memory, and that iPhone could understand voice inputs. He demonstrated a couple of questions and responses, and entranced, Della and I chose the higher-priced option.

Naturally we qualified for the deal, and we took an option limiting us to 5000 text messages a month. After we paid, I said, "Okay, Rusty, now we want to get a hotspot to use this phone."

et al.

"Oh," he said, "You'll have go to AT&T for that. They have a kiosk in the mall."

We walked out of the store with a new iPhone and spotted an AT&T sign. A nice young man with a short growth of black beard and a leather jacket offered to help. He just got started into applying for our hotspot and got stuck. He said, ""Kelly is going to have to do this."

Kelly was probably the reason the young man was hanging at the kiosk. She was an attractive, young woman wearing a tight blouse that exposed ample cleavage. A pack of Camel cigarettes poked from out her tweed sport coat pocket. After finishing up with another customer, she quickly enabled the hotspot function on our new iPhone at a cost of $45 per month. She assured us we could cancel it at the end of 3 months when we would be back by our own wireless source in Minnesota.

"Kelly, you are very good," I said in parting.

"Not all the time," said Kelly with a carnal leer.

"Jim, you bring out the best in people," Della whispered as we left.

We returned to our rental car and made it back to our condo, but not without missing a turn and going two miles out of our way. I couldn't wait to connect to our hotspot.

The first thing I did after plugging the iPhone into the Mac was to use the voice feature in the iPhone. "Hotspot," I spoke into the phone as clearly as possible. On the computer screen came a listing of nearby late-night bars where one might expect to find companions of the opposite sex (or maybe the same sex or both sexes, this was California).

Since that wasn't much help, at least for the present, I called AT&T technical support. After three ten-minute transfers, a man with a country bumpkin accent verified that the hotspot was functioning on the iPhone, but he wasn't able to help me connect to the Mac. He suggested trying every one of the twenty wireless signals that the Mac recognized. This I did over the next half hour, but none of them would open without a password.

I phoned Mac technical support next. After 45 minutes of wrong departments and waiting, a young man answered and asked for the serial number of our iPhone. He had trouble hearing, so I increased my volume. He said, "I'm sorry, but my earphones are not working right, so you will have to speak up." I spoke so loudly then that he could probably have heard me by sticking his head out his window. I got so irritated by the third attempt at yelling numbers and letters that when it came to G, I said, "G like God," and at D, I said, "D like Damn." If there had been an F, I don't think I would have used Foxtrot.

After spurious periods of silence while he leafed through technical manuals, the Mac technical specialist determined that I would have to install iTunes, and that our Mac was new enough that it should work.

et al.

"How do I install iTunes without internet access?" I queried.

"You'll have to go where there's a connection," he said. He volunteered to email some instructions on how to complete the installation of iTunes, and then how to complete the hotspot connection.

"Great," I said. "Do you think I can make it work?"

"Well, I dunno. I could. But of course, I'm a techie" he replied.

I decided that five and one-half hours of this was enough. Della and I left the condo to eat supper at a Mexican restaurant. She ordered a full rack of ribs, ate half, and doggie-bagged the rest. I had eight calamari chunks the size of large asparagus stalks and a chili relleno, a large green pepper split and stuffed with about a quarter pound of chicken meat along with cheese and veggies. I did my best to lick my platter clean, but I couldn't get around it all.

After returning to the condo, I turned on both the Mac and the new phone, and there was iPhone listed on optional wireless networks on the computer screen. Strange it wasn't there before. *Click click*, and we had internet access using a hotspot, even without iTunes installed.

That night, I tossed and turned. Mad scientists turned electronics gadgets into monsters with blinking red LEDs for eyes. They chased me, then surrounded me and taunted me. Must have been something I ate.

Memorial Weekend

J SCANNED THE FADED and wrinkled phone list trying to find my PhD advisor's number. Many on the list had died, but I hadn't the heart to cross out their names because, in a sense, it would erase them from memory. Finally, I found Dr. Hall's number. Hadn't talked to him in three years. Hope this number works.

"Hello."

"Hi Art. This is Jim Daughton."

"Oh hi, Jim. Good to hear from you."

"Are you and Ruth going to be in town the Tuesday after Memorial Day?"

"Yes, we don't plan to leave Ames. What brings you down?"

"Della and I are taking a Memorial weekend trip. Sunday we are visiting my hometown for a high school reunion, and then we will go to Maryville, Missouri to visit with my brother and sister. We are coming back from there on Tuesday and would like to

et al.

have lunch with you if you are available. We can be at your house about 11:45. We'll call when we get close."

"Sounds great. We'll be ready."

"We are interested in your family news. Della and I were saddened to learn of the death of Jane."

"Yes, ovarian cancer took her quickly. The good news is the rest of the family is doing well. We can talk about it over lunch on Tuesday."

"I am also looking forward to catching up on the news at Iowa State—both about professors and fellow students."

"We are all getting older, but I should have some of the info you're looking for."

"See you Tuesday."

ON SUNDAY BEFORE MEMORIAL Day, our Jaguar sped south down I35 past the Iowa border toward our first destination of the weekend, Grand River, Iowa. That small, southern Iowa town was home from 1946 through my college years. I belong to the fourth generation of Daughtons living in or near Grand River.

"Della, good of you to come on a trip that is mostly about me— my boyhood home, my siblings, my college."

"I am looking forward to seeing your family and Art and Ruth. Let's have fun."

A green interstate sign read 'Grand River 7 miles, Kansas City 165 miles.' We turned onto a dusty gravel road and eventually crossed the Grand River, a muddy stream about twenty feet wide. In my youth a wooden water tank stood on its bank for supplying water to steam locomotives. The tank is now gone, and so are the railway tracks that used to run through town.

When I first moved there, the population was 450 souls, and it had a bank, two grocery stores, three filling stations, a post office, lumber yard, feed store, and a combination furniture store and funeral parlor. My Methodist church was one of four houses of worship, and a three-story brick school, which my father had attended, and had also served me, my brother, Bruce, and my sister, Sheila. The Methodist Church and the school had both been leveled - not a brick remained.

Due to the revolution in agriculture, one farmer can cultivate 3,000 acres of land now compared to only 160 acres when I was a child. The main economic purpose of Grand River was to support the surrounding agriculture community whose population had radically reduced. Consequently, Grand River had shrunk to fewer than one hundred residents, and most of the remaining houses and buildings were in poor condition. The only signs of business were two beer joints/restaurants, a small post office, and a community building on the site where the school once stood. A pay-at-the-pump, self-operated gasoline station is four miles away.

et al.

The only town improvements since my youth were the black-toppings of the two crossing main streets. In the 1940s cars often got stuck there after a heavy rain. A hand pump at the intersections of the main streets had offered pails of water to businesses for those willing to pump and willing to trust the water quality. The pump was now gone.

When I was young, it was easy to forecast the deterioration of the Grand River economy. Those who stayed behind had a good life, but generally earned meager incomes. My brother, sister, and I had escaped.

As Della and I drove through town, we breezed past Daughton Street, named for my grandmother, Alice Daughton, who was once the only female postmaster in Iowa. We passed the little six-acre farmstead where the five people in my family had moved after Dad got out of the Navy. The 500-square foot, white-clapboard house was heated by an oil stove located at its center. In the winter it also served as a slow cooker for pots of ham-bones and beans, vegetable and beef stew, or pork neck-bones with potatoes, onions, and sauerkraut.

Mom's kitchen had barely enough floor space for a pirouette, yet she cooked big family meals and canned hundreds of quarts of vegetables and meat each year. A dipper from a water pail relieved our thirst. Three very small bedrooms belonged to Sheila, Mom and Dad, and Bruce and me. A full-sized bed left almost no walking space in ours, but later a bunk bed gave us a little more space. The rest of the house held a dining room table, a few chairs, and two very large wooden bookcases full of books. The toilet was a two-holer about 100 feet out the back-porch door.

A garage, chicken house, outdoor fruit cellar, and barn completed the structures on the acreage. We raised chickens, pigs, and sheep. We milked two or three cows, churned butter, and made cottage cheese. A half-acre garden, fifty fruit trees, and an asparagus bed combined with hunting and fishing gave us most of what we ate.

Although far from opulent, our little farmstead was as neat as a pin.

As we drove alongside my old house, I tried to peek through brush to see what was left but could see only traces of an old dilapidated and deserted trailer. All traces of the house, garage, and chicken house were completed obscured. I had heard few years ago that the barn had been struck by lighting and burned. The former weed-free bluegrass pasture was now covered with trees and brush. It was all I could do to keep from crying.

"Well, Della, now we have a job to do. We have to put flowers on my parents' and grandparents' graves."

We drove about half a mile further to the Grand River Cemetery. Peonies by the entrance were still bright and fragrant. By some tombstones, The Stars and Stripes flew from wooden sticks to honor Veteran's Day of ex-servicemen, including my father. My parents and grandparents were buried in adjacent gravesites along the road. They hadn't had flowers for the past three years, but grass was well trimmed around the headstones. With the flowers we put there, visitors would now know they were remembered.

A row of tall pine trees once lined the north side of the graveyard. As a boy I would climb up into the branches and listen to the needles purr softly in the breeze. Red-winged blackbirds unaware of my presence would sit near me and sing. I wondered then if the dead could sense this pleasant scene. I now walked to where the pines once stood but found only stumps six inches high.

We exited the cemetery to the left the rickety, old Daughton Rodeo Pavilion, named for my cousin John, and re-entered the town passing the lot where the Methodist Church once stood. I could remember hearing hymns, seeing colored beams stream through the stained-glass windows, eating fabulous harvest dinners, feeling the sadness of my family funerals, the joy of my sister's marriage, and the pride in my high school graduation ceremony. There was nothing physical to mark where these once took place. I had memories, but an emptiness came over me. Were these memories real or made up?

I graduated from Grand River High School in 1954, my brother in 1957, and my sister in 1958. Two years after that there was no high school in Grand River, but every year since there had been a reunion for anyone who had ever attended, with a special class recognition for those celebrating a 50th year. My sister wasn't attending, even though it was her 50th, but my brother was to come from Billings, MT. Della and I parked among the dusty pickups by the community center and walked through the front door to register and pay ten dollars each as entry fees. The meal was catered by Hy-Vee.

The lady who'd been organizing these events could not attend due to fluid on her lungs. She was valedictorian of my class. I took her to our senior prom even though she was engaged to a Grand River boy who was away in the Navy. I bought her an orchid corsage. Ours was a date of convenience as I had no girlfriend. I don't remember a goodnight kiss.

Brother Bruce arrived, and after a short conversation with Della and me, he joined a table with four other 1957 graduates.

I talked to most of the fifty people at the center, but only one other person from my class came. He was toothless and fat. He could have passed for a smaller version of Jabba the Hut. Only four of the twelve members of my graduating class still live.

"Hey, cousin, do you remember eating boiled radishes?" I asked a wiry redheaded man. "My dad remembered eating them at your grandfather's house about 1925."

"Hell yes, Jim. I guess we're the only family that still eats them." Dick had married the prettiest girl in Grand River, and she was taking entry fees at the door. He'd made Brigadier General in the Air Force, and a few years ago had managed to get a squadron flyover of the Grand River cemetery on Memorial Day. Dick is now full of cancer, fighting for his life.

et al.

Della and I endured about an hour of group administrivia, told Bruce we'd meet him at our sister's home, and headed for the home of Sheila and Alfred Smith in Maryville, Missouri, about ninety miles distant.

THE TWO OF US unpacked at the Holiday Inn and were surprised by upgrades in the furniture and bathroom since our last stay. We drove across town to the small, two-story Smith home and hugged Sheila and shook hands with Al. Soon after had we parked, Bruce came and parked in the driveway beside the Jaguar. The five of us sat in the living room and exchanged updates on children and grandchildren.

"Al, your life has really changed. This is the first year in the past forty your aren't teaching."

"Forty-two years, Jim. But it's not a bad change for me. The past several years I've hated teaching at Northwest Missouri State."

"The students just aren't the same," said Sheila. "It used to be the students really wanted to learn and were willing to work hard. Al was 'Professor the Year' for ten straight years. Now the student's goal is to get an A with the least work possible. Learning is secondary."

"My philosophy of teaching is at odds with the students' philosophy of learning. We are incompatible. It is just as well I am no longer involved," said Al.

"How are you doing, Bruce?" asked Sheila.

"Pretty well," said Bruce. "I miss Mary Pat terribly. But I find things to do. I sing in the church choir, visit members of our old MS support group and friends in nursing homes, play bridge, and I've taken up playing golf again."

"You've driven to see your grandchildren, too," I said.

"Yes. I drove to California to see Dan, to Washington to see Kay, and to New Mexico to see Bill and to see Bridget graduate from college. And I drove back here to see you and to attend my high school reunion. But life isn't as good without Mary Pat."

"Are you really going to buy a new house, Sheila?" asked Bruce. "You have talked about it for years."

"I just can't climb the stairs many more years. We have to do something, but I just can't find what I want in Maryville, and I don't want to move out of the city. So we just keep looking."

"How about a pitch game?" asked Al.

"Good idea," said Bruce.

Al got out a card table, score pad, and a deck of cards. Bruce and Al played partners against Sheila and me. Shelia, Bruce, and

et al.

I had played the game since about first grade. Della lay down on the couch and read.

After a couple hours of card playing, Sheila announced, "Time for supper." We sat down to a sumptuous meal. Included was Sheila's last asparagus of the year from her garden. Also included was her last package of frozen 'Samantha Warwick' beans, named for a Danish pioneer who settled near Grand River in the 19th century. The whole pods were cooked after they were filled with maturing beans, and they tasted better than any other variety. Seed had been passed down from generation-to-generation in Grand River, and Sheila received hers from our father.

"Sheila, that was a great meal," I sighed.

"Everything was super," agreed Della.

"Let's get back to the pitch game," Sheila said. "Jim and I have a little catching up to do."

The game lasted until 9:00 PM. Bruce went to bed upstairs, and Della and I returned to the Holiday Inn for a good night's sleep.

THE MORNING OF MEMORIAL Day, Della and I had a good self-service breakfast in the motel and then drove back to the Smith's home. Al and Sheila had eaten and Bruce was finishing a light breakfast in the kitchen. We gathered in the living room.

"Sheila, you never go to the reunion," remarked Bruce. "An honors table was set for your class of 1958, but you weren't there, and no one else from your class was either."

"My three best friends in my class have died. When I came back from college, I didn't have much in common with the others. And unlike you and Jim, I am not saddened by how our old house has gone to the dogs. It's just gone. Part of the past, the way life goes. No nostalgia for me. Must not be much for my classmates still living either."

"I probably won't go again. The attendance is way down and I don't get enough out of it," Bruce said.

"I feel the same at this stage of my life," I remarked.

"You two are catching on to why I don't go," Sheila chimed in.

"You're a hard case, Sis," I said. "But you are still my partner in pitch. Let's clean up on Bruce and Al. We have gone far too easy on them."

"Agreed on that, at least," said Sheila.

We played cards the rest of the day taking a time-out only to eat fabulous meals prepared by Sheila. When it approached bedtime, Bruce said, "I will probably be gone when you and Della come back tomorrow. I want to get a good start to Montana." So we said our goodbyes and hugged, holding back tears.

et al.

DELLA AND I RETURNED to the Holiday Inn for another night's sleep, and for another breakfast the following morning. The Tuesday after Memorial Day we returned to the Smith house. Bruce had already left.

"He left before we got up at 5AM," said Sheila. She had a couple of snacks prepared for our ride home.

"How do you think he's adjusting to the loss of Mary Pat?" Della asked.

"In one sense you would think he would feel freer," I ventured. "He was her cook, house cleaner, launderer, nurse, trainer, chauffeur, and physical therapist for over thirty years, but he never minded caring for her because he loved her so much. Now he believes they will be reunited in heaven when he dies, and he actually looks forward to that day."

Sheila said, "You're right, Jim. In a way, he's now just going through the motions—day by day. I hope he can discover some joy in the life he has left."

"That would be a good wish for all of us," said Al.

Della and I climbed in the Jaguar and headed north to Ames, Iowa.

"DELLA, YOU MAY NOT appreciate how important Dr. Hall was to my life. Art was an icon in the field of thin magnetic films, and he adopted me as a graduate student and gave me an assistantship that paid my way through graduate school. I basked in the wake of his brilliance through graduate school and for thirty years thereafter during joint research with him. My career was what it was largely due to him."

"He really likes you, Jim. Art and Ruth are such nice people, too."

About 11:00 AM we arrived at the outskirts of Ames and phoned the Halls. "We'll be out front when you get here," said Ruth.

They were ready and waiting in front of their townhouse when we arrived. After exchanging greetings, Art said, 'Why don't you follow our car to the restaurant? Then you can continue back to Minneapolis after you've eaten"

"Good idea," I said.

We followed them for a few miles to The Café, and we were soon seated at a booth for four. For the next hour we heard about people I knew at Iowa State, who had died and who were still living. My classmate—also the best man at my first marriage—was still active, and he spent much of his time at a cabin built on Lake Vermillion. Most of my professors had passed on.

"I notice from the department newsletter that a majority of the current teachers have Indian and Chinese surnames," I said.

et al.

"It's very different now than when you went here," Art agreed. "There are very few US-born staffers now."

"Is that for good or bad?" I asked.

"Neither. It just is. The world has changed. But we sure remember the good times when you were a student."

The conversation turned to family. "Jane's death must have been a shock," said Della.

"Yes," agreed Ruth. "Her son by her ex-husband is now doing all right. Did you know Jane had a wife? She is doing OK as well." Della and I exchanged glances. Neither of us pursued the subject.

"How are your daughter and son-in-law doing in the veterinarian business?" I asked.

"Fantastic. Their practice is growing and our granddaughter who just became a vet is now joining them," said Ruth.

"Boy, this food is good." I said.

"We believe it's the best Ames has to offer," said Art. "Glad you like it."

We finished our meal, said goodbye to the Halls, and headed back to Minnesota.

"THOSE TWO HAVE HARDLY changed since we saw them three years ago," remarked Della. "They sure don't look ninety-three years old. Her skin is so smooth. I wish we can look as good as they do when we are ninety-three."

"Thank you for coming with me these past three days, Della. The trip was mostly for me. It brought back so many memories, mostly good ones, but I guess you can't really go back. It's not there anymore."

"Memories get stronger when shared with people you like and love, Jim. And maybe that's enough."

"I guess that will have to do."

Getting Old Sucks

"GETTING OLD SUCKS," I said as I set my duffle bag full of dirty clothes through the front door into our apartment.

"That's fine greeting after being gone for three days," said Joan. "Did you catch fish?"

"Yep. That part of the trip went okay."

"Well then, what's the problem?"

"I peed in Bob's boat."

"What? That boat is our boy's pride and joy. How in the hell did that happen?"

"It's kind of a long story. Let's sit down and I'll tell you."

"OK. But we better sit by the kitchen table. I'll clean the seat of your wooden chair after the mess those fishing pants will make."

After we sat, Joan poured out two cups of coffee and sat across from me.

et al.

"You know it was pretty cold out there on Lake Sharpe, a high of 45 degrees air temperature with a water temperature of 37 degrees. My circulation isn't so good anymore, so I had to wear a lot of clothes. My Cabella guide-wear suit, jacket and pants, long wool underwear (tops and bottoms), and regular underwear under all that."

"So you had to get through a lot of layers when you had to pee."

"You're getting the idea. Actually, I usually try to avoid the problem by waiting until we go ashore. That didn't used to be a problem, but my pee capacity has declined since my bladder got radiated while its neighbor, the cancerous prostate, got obliterated. Getting old sucks. This day I was holding on with all my will but knew I just couldn't wait to reach shore. I unzipped the top of my Cabella suit, and still sitting down, managed to zip up the fly on the bottom of the suit."

"Just a few more layers to go," said Joan.

"I had to stand up, and the boat was rocking so much I had to use one hand to hold a gunnel to steady myself. With the other hand, cold and shaking, I had to find the fly of my pants and zip it down. After that, the fly on the wool underwear was not aligned with the fly on the pants. But by squirming this way and that, I reached the shorts."

"And still you held your pee?"

"Yes, but it was perilous. I never had to pee that bad in my life. And worse was to come. I couldn't locate the fly on the shorts. My only way to get the wiener out was out through the leg."

"I'll bet getting it out through all those layers was a challenge."

"As you know, Sweet Joan, I am not super-endowed in the penile area, and the cold weather made things all the more difficult. Finally, I managed to hold the end of my penis between my thumb and forefinger and guide a pee stream over the edge of the boat and into the lake. What a relief!"

"All's well that ends well,"

"Then a wave caused the boat to lurch, and my grip slipped a little. The bottom of the leg of my shorts caused the urine stream to spray on the inside wall of the boat. Not a lot, but enough to see."

"What did you do?"

"I tucked everything back into place and washed my hand in the lake. Then I told Bob."

"What did he say?"

"At first he looked irked. But then he said it was all right. He said I had cleaned up after him when he was a boy, so it was just payback time."

"Did that make it okay?"

et al.

"Not really. He knew he has to take care of me. Our relationship has changed. I didn't want him to think he has to take care of me."

"We have a good boy."

"Yes, we do. But getting old sucks.

Aisha and Conrad

"IT'S BEEN AN INTERESTING day, Conrad."

"That's good to hear, Aisha, my pet."

Dinner hour was finished in Sunny Hills Nursing Home. Dirty dishes had been returned to the kitchen, but the odor of tuna casserole hung in the air. Aisha preferred her door be shut so her conversations with her husband could be more private. She sat in a recliner next to her bed. The setting sun sent a beam across the room, highlighting a few suspended dust particles in its path. A red, white, and blue Afghan she had knitted herself was spread over her lap and legs.

"My new friend, Darlene, came for an hour this morning before I had my hair done. And this afternoon I won bingo three times. Isn't that something?"

"It sure is, Dear."

"It's starting to snow again. Remember when it snowed at our wedding?"

et al.

"I sure do. How could I forget?"

"My mother arrived an hour late. Everyone sat so patiently in the church. Finally, we had to go ahead with the service. Mom got there just after we left the altar. Do you remember that?"

"I remember that well, Aisha. It was December 20, 1964. That was the day Levi Eshkol formed the twelfth Israeli government."

"Have you heard the weather? Will this be a bad storm?" she asked.

"My little chickadee, there will be snow flurries tonight, but tomorrow and Friday will be sunny, but a little frigid with highs in the 30's and lows in the single digits."

"Brrrr. I guess I'm glad to be in here where it's warm and comfortable."

A nurse's aide knocked and entered. "It's time for your meds, Aisha."

"Oh, if I must. Here, I already have a glass of water." She looked at the three pills, a big pink one she called a 'horse choker' because of its size, but she didn't know what it was for. Anyway, she swallowed them all at once. The nursing home worker recorded the administration of medicine and left the room.

Aisha's swatted her hand at an invisible bug. "Those damned floaters have been a nuisance today. I see black spots flying across in front of me. I know they aren't real, but they are a bother. Conrad, I wonder what causes them?"

"My Darling, eye floaters are images formed by deposits of protein drifting about in the vitreous, the clear, jelly-like substance that fills the middle of the eye. They seem to drift in front of the eye, but they do not block vision. The floater is a result of debris from the vitreous casting a shadow on the retina."

"Conrad, you are a virtual fount of knowledge."

"Nice of you to say so, Aisha."

"You know, Conrad, we've heard in the last week from Nancy and Ruth, but I don't think we have heard from Martha for a while. Has Martha sent an email?"

"On January 20th Martha emailed you. Would you like me to read it to you, Dear?"

"Please do, Conrad."

Dear Mom,

Sorry I haven't written sooner. Having been a mother yourself, I bet you understand that three children can keep you very busy.

You would be so proud to see how well Sam can play the piano. Bill has been getting top grades in his class, and little Aida is so cute. She loves to dress up in my clothes,

> *which just hang on her. My husband is now a vice president, and he travels a good deal which leaves me a virtual single parent much of the time.*
>
> *If we can break free next summer, maybe we can drive back east to see you. You will be just amazed to see your grandchildren. If Dad were still alive, I know he would be amazed, too...*

"STOP, STOP. DON'T READ any more," screamed Aisha. "I don't want to be reminded that you died." She sobbed spasmodically.

"I'm sorry you are upset, Aisha. I should have been programmed to filter out references to my death."

The room went silent with Aisha slumped in her chair until another knock sounded at the door. An LPN entered. "It's almost quiet time, Aisha. Let's get you over to bed."

After tucking her in, she carefully placed the iPad Pro7 on her nightstand, making sure the charger was plugged in. She dimmed the room lights. "Good night, Aisha."

Aisha, still choking back tears, replied, "Good night, Beth."

Now she remembered what the pink pill was for. "Anxiety," the doctor had said. She reached over and put her hand on the iPad, which was receiving new life through the power cord. A faded color photograph of she and Conrad and their small children sat on the nightstand. The glass covering the picture had cracked two years ago when she finally left her home of forty years to move to Sunny Hills. She fell asleep.

BETH MET ANN, A co-worker, outside the door. "Is there a problem with Aisha?"

"When she realizes that her husband really isn't in the room, she gets depressed for a while. She'll be all right in the morning and start talking to Conrad again."

"Are you and Bill going to get 'life-profiled' so you can keep in touch after one of you dies?" asked Beth.

"Oh, I dunno," said Ann. "It would take a week out of our lives and cost thousands, even in the economical workshop mode. What a project. And then you have to get updated from time to time. It's supposed to take some of the sting out of loneliness for the surviving spouse, but maybe we'll wait until we are a little older. How about you and John?"

"Not sure we're going to do it. It may help some, but we wonder if it just stretches out the grieving process. Maybe it'd be better to just face reality. We'll see in a few years."

Section C:

Fishing &

Fishing Friends

Getting Away

*J*OHN AND HIS SON Max wandered among booths at the Winter Sportsman's Show. The thirteen-year-old's jaw dropped as he viewed pictures of large walleyed pike taken at various resorts from around Minnesota and Canada. "Wow, Dad. Wouldn't it be great to go to one of these places this spring?"

"Sure would be, Son." But John feared it wouldn't be possible with the temporary divorce settlement likely to become final in the next few months. After support for Betty, Max and his sisters, and all other fixed payments, he had only six-hundred dollars a month for food, gas, and other expenses.

They approached a small booth sitting off by itself. "Hi. I'm Ken Hendrickson and this is my wife Donna. Would you boys be looking for a place to go fishing this spring?" In the couple's booth hung pictures of TeepeeTonka Resort—lakeside cabins surrounded by tall pine trees, an orange and red sunset over a wind-rippled lake, and happy fishermen holding stringers of big fish. No other potential customers were hanging around the Hendricksons' booth. Theirs looked similar to the others, but there was something more open and friendlier about these people.

"I'm John and this is my son Max. Where is Blackduck Lake, anyway?"

"Near a town in Minnesota of the same name. About forty miles northeast of Bemidji. We bought this resort last year after I got hurt working for the highway department. Couldn't do that road stuff anymore. We spent most of the past year fixing the place to open this spring." John noticed a metal brace fitted along Ken's back.

"Got any openings the first week of the season?"

"No," said Donna, "we are full. But we have some openings the following week."

"Our finances are a little limited at this time, but we might be interested," said John.

Donna gave Ken a knowing look, and he nodded back.

"We might have just the thing," said Ken. "It's a ninety-five-dollar weekend special, three nights in a cabin, Friday through Sunday, and it includes a fourteen-foot boat. Just show up on Friday at the end of the first week of the season."

"Oh, please Dad. Can we go?" Max asked.

John saw looked down at his son. He hesitated. "OK, we'll do it," said John. "Do you need a deposit?"

"No," said Donna. "Just pay when you come."

They grabbed a brochure, and John carefully recorded Ken's directions to the resort on it – 94 west to 24 north to 10 east to 371 to 2 east to 29 north to Blackduck and 71 north and west at the filling station and north one block just past the golf course to the lake, and a quarter mile past the Hilltop Restaurant to TeepeeTonka Resort.

On their way back to his townhome, John said, "This will give us something to look forward to, huh Max?"

"I'll dream about the trip every night."

JOHN LEFT THE TURMOIL of work at 4:00 PM after packing up two fat manila folders full of documents. One concerned the split of his Honeywell division between the Plymouth and Colorado Springs locations and the other, the largest Department of Defense program ever bid by his company. Interdivisional squabbles had degenerated into character assassinations. Several top executives opposing John's views had threatened to get him fired. He hoped being away for a few days might relieve the pressure of work.

Back at his townhome he loaded the Ford Explorer with fishing gear, snacks, groceries, and clothing for their trip to Blackduck. He pulled up to his former residence and picked up Max who stood waiting outside with a small suitcase. His mother was barking last minute instructions into his ear. John's daughters peeked out through a window but made no move to come outside to greet him. He smiled and waved, but they didn't respond. When Betty went inside, the girls left the window.

John hugged Max. "Hi, Son. How was school today?"

"Good."

"Are you excited about our trip?"

"Boy, am I?" Max grinned from ear to ear.

"By the way, did you have any supper?"

"Yeah. Mom gave me mac and cheese and an apple."

"There're potato chips, salami, and a can of Coke under the front seat. When you get hungry, help yourself. We've got a long drive ahead."

"Let's get going. I can't wait to go fishing."

"Hop in. It'll be a rainy ride." Max got in the front seat of the Explorer and strapped on his seat belt. It was almost 5:00 PM.

John stuck Ken Hendrickson's driving instructions beside him, and they were off.

"Your mother didn't seem too happy back there."

"She's mad about the divorce settlement. She thinks she got cheated."

"She's the one who wanted a divorce, not me. I didn't bribe the judge."

"I know it, Dad. Let's stop talking about it."

"She also wants you to spend more than two nights a week at her house. What do you think of that?"

"I like things the way they are."

"Me, too. You can spend as much time with me as you want."

There was no problem getting to 494 and 94 except for the traffic snarls involving half of Minneapolis headed to the lakes on a Friday evening. Rain beat against the windshield accompanying by lightning strikes and thunder.

"Do you really think we'll catch fish, Dad?"

"Yeah, I'll bet we will. When I was a boy, we caught fish in northern Minnesota this time of year. We should do all right."

It was not an easy trip. The windshield wipers couldn't completely clear the pouring rain. Low-hanging black clouds made it nearly dark as night in the late afternoon. After sunset it was worse. Near Blackduck they turned onto a narrow, blacktopped road with the tops of evergreen limbs hanging over its edges. By now it was really creepy. One deer, and then two more behind the first, dashed in front of them. Lighting strikes provided brief, but brilliant illumination.

Finally, they reached the town of Backduck. John pulled into the gas station and asked the attendant, "How do I get to TeepeeTonka Resort?"

"Just follow that road to the lake and take a left. Not the first one to the lake access, but the second left. It's just a little way from there."

As they pulled up to the resort, the rain let up a bit. Ken was in a large and lighted garage working on a lawnmower. He wiped the grease off his hands and greeted them. "Hi John. Hi Max." Park your vehicle over by number 8. I have the electric heat on. Make yourself at home. You're staying until Monday, right?"

"Yep. Luckily my son's school is having teachers' conferences, so we should even be able to fish awhile on Monday."

They unloaded the SUV taking care to put milk, eggs, and bacon in the refrigerator. Father and son fell to sleep soon after crawling into the twin beds. A light rain pelted the windows of the cabin. It was 11:00 PM.

FIRST, JOHN HEARD THE red-winged blackbirds singing of territories and matings, and then he opened his eyes to a bright dawn. Just outside the bedroom window noisy birds perched on last year's cattails that rose over green shoots of this spring's new crop. The lake was smooth as glass and the blue sky was clear except for a few cotton balls. John's Timex said 4:45.

Careful not to wake Max, he shut the bedroom door behind him and prepared breakfast—Tang, bacon, and toast. He would scramble the eggs after Max woke up.

With a little time on his hands, he decided to look through those business folders. He didn't remember bringing them in last night, so he looked in the Explorer. Nothing. Could it be? Could he have left them back at the duplex on the kitchen table? Damn! He wouldn't be able to work on them until Monday evening. Nothing to be done until then. Business will have to wait.

John walked out of the cabin toward the dock. The cool, fresh air smelled of lilacs and pines. It was as though he had entered a new slower and simpler world. Ken was already working on the boats. "Good morning, John. Sure is a beautiful morning after that storm. Max ready to go fishing?"

"Still sleeping, but not for long. He'll be raring to go."

et al.

"Your boat is over here at Number 8. I could rent you a motor at fifty dollars a day. You interested?"

"Max and I fish some in the Cities, and we manage by rowing. We'll be okay with oars. Is there any place we can fish nearby without having to go two miles across the lake?"

"If I was you, I would row around the shore to the south, just by the Hilltop. Fish in about eight feet of water. Move around a little if you're not having any luck."

"Where do I get some minnows?"

"There's the minnow tank. Just write in the book as you take them. It's fifty cents a scoop. You can pay for them when you settle up."

"Thanks, Ken."

"Good luck fishing. By the way, if you need to make a call, you can use the phone in the office."

"Don't think it'll be necessary. There won't be anyone in my office until Monday, and we'll be starting back then. I'd better see if Max's awake."

Max was up and dressed. "Let's get going, Dad."

"First you have to eat breakfast. It's already except for the eggs, and they will be done in a few minutes."

After eating breakfast and stacking dirty dishes in the sink, they collected their spinning rods and a tackle box, grabbed a landing net and a minnow bucket with three scoops of minnows from the boathouse, and boarded their aluminum boat. John rowed away from the dock and headed down the shoreline by the Hilltop. The boat was big and heavy and a little awkward to row, but John managed to arrive directly offshore from the restaurant.

Six ducks flew overhead making whistling noises to the beat of their wings. "Those are American Golden Eyes, otherwise known as whistlers. The drakes have a loose wing feather that makes the sound. We're going to see lots of water birds today: loons, mallards, teal, wood ducks, bluebills, grebes, and coots. I'll point them out."

"Let's start fishing. How do we know where to go?" asked Max.

"Ken said to fish in about eight feet of water."

"I can see the bottom of the lake, but how will we know how deep we're fishing?"

"Max, you see this anchor rope. I will drop this anchor until it hits bottom. I will raise the anchor and see how much line is out. When I spread my arms, the distance between my hands is about six feet. I can guess at the other two feet pretty well."

John rowed out beyond where new reeds were poking out of the water and dropped anchor. It needed only four feet of rope to hit bottom. He rowed out further and tried again. This time, they were in about eight feet.

John tied hooks onto the monofilament lines on their spinning reels and tied a lead sinker about eight inches above the hook. Then he put minnows on the hooks. "OK, Max, let your line down to within a few inches of bottom. Let's see if we can catch a fish. And be quiet. The water is clear and shallow, the fish will be easy to spook."

They didn't have long to wait. Max saw the tip of his rod dance, and he reeled in a fifteen-inch walleye. He pumped his fist and beamed. "My first walleye!"

John smiled. He knew this would be one of the moments that would live in their memories.

Every few minutes they pulled in a nice eating-size walleye—fourteen to sixteen inches long. John netted their fish, stuck them on the stringer, and untangled Max's line when he had problems, which happened frequently.

Other fishermen must have had binoculars and noticed they were catching fish. Boats would motor up near them and splash down anchors. After ten minutes of catching nothing, and ruining the fishing for John and Max, too, they would motor away. Ten minutes after the intruders left, the fish would bite again.

"Max, I'm afraid we have our limit, twelve. We can eat a few and come back later."

"Dad, this has been great, but do we have to go in?"

"We could 'catch and release' fish—say we are fishing for other kinds of fish. But I think we should go in and clean the fish we've caught."

John rowed back to the dock, and he let Max carry the stringer of twelve walleyes, which was almost too heavy for him to lift. Donna spied him and rushed down with a Polaroid camera. "Boy, that's the best catch this spring. Hey, Ken. Come see what Max caught."

"Oh, wow," said Ken. "Aren't you proud of your catch?"

"I suppose so," said a beaming Max. "But now that we have our limits, we can't fish anymore."

"You've had better luck that any of our other customers. I'm sure the less fortunate would be glad to take some of the fish off your hands. Then you could fish some more."

"Would that be legal?" asked John.

"Consider it group fishing limits for campers at Teepee Tonka. If they don't exceed their possession limits, everything is legal."

et al.

"Great. I'll clean them and give you ten to distribute. I'll save just two fish for Max and me for lunch. Then Max and I can go catch ten more."

John and Max continued to out-fish their fellow campers the rest of Saturday and all of Sunday. The secret was most likely their inability to afford a loud, noisy motor to fish in clear, shallow water.

THEY PACKED THE CAR on Monday morning after one last visit to their fishing spot. Max waited in the Ford, strapped into the copilot's seat. John went to the office. "Donna, I guess it's time to settle up."

"I have your bill all ready made out. Look it over for any mistakes."

John wrote out a check and handed it to her. "I can't tell you how much we enjoyed our stay here. It's been pretty rough back home. Divorces are tough on children."

"On dads, too. Any other children?"

"Yeah, two girls. I see my daughters only briefly every two weeks. Max is all the family I have left. But do you know what? I am blessed. He is enough. At least for now. The girls will come around."

"Good luck to you and Max. Hope to see you back next year."

John and Max had a fishing trip to remember. Tuesday before the school bus came, John delivered Max to his mother's house. Only then did he open the folders he had left on the kitchen table.

Two Thousand Sixteen

"*H*OP IN, DAD. LET'S go fishing," said Max. He had driven to the retirement home in a black Ford 150 pickup trailering a sparkling new nineteen-foot Ranger motorboat.

"Back to TepeeTonka after all these years," said John. "I'll miss the Hendricksons. You say they sold the resort?"

"Yeah, to a young couple. I talked to her when I made the reservation. Seems very nice. Price has gone up a bit. Three hundred bucks for the weekend. What did we pay that first weekend?"

"Ninety-five dollars. But I'll bet you can afford the three hundred now more than I could the ninety-five then. By the way, congratulations on your promotion to vice president. How's the company doing, anyway?"

et al.

"It's absolutely insane. The whole atmosphere is toxic. You wouldn't believe the backbiting. Everyone's unhappy. It should do me some good to get away from it all on a fishing trip with you."

"What's your territory now?"

"Basically, it's all of the northern states. Keeps me hopping. My office could be anywhere. It's wherever my phone and computer are. I have to travel a lot, too. But I always try to be at home on Friday and the weekend."

They drove off toward Blackduck Lake. It was 6:00 am.

"Do you remember the way?" asked John.

"I think I remember, but not to worry. This vehicle has a navigation system. I typed in the address for TepeeTonka, and the screen will direct us all the way to Blackduck Lake. And the route selected for the shortest driving time. Are you ready for breakfast?"

"Sure. How about you?"

"I'm ready. My cell phone will find a good eatery along the way." Max typed a few strokes and then stared at the display. "Looks like the Copper Kettle in Clearwater has good reviews."

"How do you do that?" asked John.

"It's an app called Yelp. It's never let me down."

They stopped at the restaurant and placed orders. As soon as the waitress left the table, Max said, "Excuse me, Dad, but I have a meeting with a problem customer."

Max went just outside the front door and made a phone call. Just as the food came, Max returned, and they ate.

After they finished a big breakfast Max said, "I don't think I will need any lunch. How about you?"

"A few snacks will tide me over until supper. That should leave the whole afternoon for fishing."

"Would you mind driving for a while? The weekly summary meeting is scheduled for 9:00, and I should have access to my computer."

"No problem," said John.

Max crawled in the backseat with phone and computer. He wore a headset and mouthpiece that left his hands free for his phone and computer. Occasionally he glanced at the pickup's console display to insure John was on the right path. Sometimes he spoke earnestly into the phone about a customer issue or about the slowness of contract preparations. Max's meeting ended as they pulled into TeepeeTonka. Tim and Carolyn greeted them in the driveway. "John and Max, welcome to our resort."

Tim looked at their boat. "That's a mighty handsome vessel, but it's probably too large to launch here. You should go back a half a mile to the city landing. That facility is plenty big enough.

et al.

And of course, you can tie up at our dock once you have the boat in the water."

"We'll help you unload," said Carolyn. "We've got you in number six."

After their groceries, clothes, and fishing gear were stowed, Max said, "Dad, I need you to drive the trailer back here after we launch over at the city ramp. I'll meet you back here with the boat."

"Let's git 'er done," said John. And they did.

After the pickup and trailer were parked by the cabin and the boat was tied up at the dock, John and Max went to the office. "Any fishing advice for us?" Max asked Tim."

"The bite's been slow. Water's is still a little cold in mid-May A few people caught some last week at the Sand Bar. Here, I'll show you where that is on the map of the lake."

"That would be helpful," said Max. "We also have a CD map of Blackduck Lake stored in our Hummingbird. A cursor marks our current GPS location."

"Wow," said Tim. "You should be able to find your way around with that thing."

"Max has every fishing gadget known to man," said John. "He's almost become a professional fisherman."

Father and son loaded their boat with snacks, a fishing net, and a bucket with six scoops of minnows. Max started the big Evinrude, and they headed for the Sandbar. "It won't take long to get there with this motor. We can go fifty mph on smooth water."

Fifteen minutes later when they arrived at the location, Max said, "Dad, this is a pretty big area. We'd better explore the water with the MinnKota trolling motor. The big motor might spook the fish. This water is clear as glass."

"So you remember that lesson learned on our first trip here?"

"Yep. But technology has improved so we don't need luck to find the fish. This Hummingbird has side-scanning sonar that can locate any fish within 200 feet of either side of our boat."

After driving around for a few minutes, Max said," there's a big pod of fish, probably walleyes, in about fifteen feet of water just off our starboard. You can almost see the bottom. We'd better anchor away from the fish and cast bobbers in to them."

"One problem, Max. There's no anchor in the boat."

"Not to worry. We have a 'spot anchor,' a GPS link to the trolling motor will keep us within five feet of where we are when I push this button. I have two bobber rigs already tied. Do you know how a slip bobber works?"

"No, please show me," said John.

et al.

"There is a small threaded knot on your monofilament line. Your bobber will ride above that knot. The knot is small enough to stay fixed to the line when you reel in. The bobber just slides up the line. I've set the bobbers to a depth of twelve feet. Cast your line about fifty feet over to where we located the school. The fish will come up from the bottom to get the bait."

John's bobber was first to go down. Max grabbed the landing net as John reeled in their first fish. Max's cell phone rang. His headset left both hands free. As Max netted a nice walleye, he said, "How about those Pirates?"

After a brief pause, Max continued, "But I think the Cubs may have better pitchers."

Another pause. "Did our demonstration convince you to go with us?"

Another pause. "We would certainly appreciate your business. If there is any further information that would help you make a decision, just ask."

Max said, "That was a customer."

"Yeah, I figured. Where's a stringer for this fish?"

"Stringers are old fashioned. Throw the walleye in the live well. A pump circulates water to keep the fish alive." He opened a hinged door over a container of water for John to aim at with the fish. Splash, Max shut the door.

Then Max's bobber went down, and he began reeling. As his fish came to the surface, a bugle sounded on his cell phone. "Holy shit, it's my boss. Could you net this fish?"

"Sure," said John.

"Hi Ray, what's happening?"

A very long pause. A concerned look clouded Max's face. "What would you like me to do?

Another pause. "I'll look over the contract tonight. I have my computer with. I should have a markup into contracts tomorrow morning."

Another pause. "You have a good weekend, too."

They spent the remainder of the afternoon reeling in fish and answering phone calls. "That was number twelve for the well," said Max, "We should go in and clean these fish."

They motored in and tied up at number six and loaded twelve nice walleyes in the landing net. Carolyn met them at the dock with a phone in hand. "That's the nicest catch this year. I just have to have a picture."

"No problem," said Max. They laid the fish side by side on a table by the boathouse. The walleyes were still flopping around and had to be constantly corralled for their portraits. "Could you use some fish?"

et al.

"Yes. Tim and I haven't had time to go fishing. We would really appreciate a few."

"We'll clean this batch and leave you some at the office," said Max.

Max with his electric knife and John with a fillet knife made quick work of dressing out the fish, one plastic bag for Tim and Carolyn and another for themselves.

"How many fillets can you eat," asked Max.

"I'm really hungry," said John. I think I can eat three."

"That sounds about right for me, too.

Soon cabin six was filled with odors of fried fish and potatoes. Supper was finished, and the dishes done just before the sun set over Blackduck Lake. "I have to work on a contract," said Max.

"That's okay," said John. "You have a job to do. I knew something like that might happen, so I brought a book to read."

About 10:00 PM John went to his bedroom. Sometime later Max turned off his computer and went to the other bedroom.

THEY WOKE SATURDAY MORNING to a light rain. John fixed a hearty breakfast of bacon, eggs, and pancakes with maple syrup. After eating Max said, "I have to talk to our contracts lady. Shouldn't take more than half an hour."

"I'm at a good place in my book. Take your time."

"Hi Shelly. Sorry to take part of your weekend. Did you get my markup?"

A short pause. "Ray didn't like Section Four. Puts our company at too great a risk. I tried to give us an escape route if everything turns to shit. What do you think?

Pause. "Glad you like it. Now get our legal beagles to approve it. The other comments are more minor and should go through. Please give me an email as soon as you know so I can tell my boss."

Pause. "You have a good weekend, too."

John and Max slipped on ponchos. "Are you going to take that phone and headset out in the rain?" asked John.

"It's a pretty light rain. I think it will be alright."

"I packed some ham sandwiches and apples for lunch," said John.

They went back to the Sandbar and caught nine walleyes on bobbers in a few hours. Phone calls punctuated the fishing action. One call notified Max that the contract was ready to go, and he

et al.

relayed that news to his boss in a half-hour conversation. Another call was good news from one of Max's salesmen.

"Hi, Bob. I saw that sale on the bulletin board. Good going, Pal. That put us way past linear to plan."

Pause. "Oh, I'm out fishing for a few days with my dad. Thought getting away could help get my mind right."

After the live well was shut on their walleye limit, Max said, "It's too early to go in, Dad. Want to try something different?"

"Sure, Max. What do you have in mind?"

Max dug out two casting rods from a side bin and attached spinner baits. "You wouldn't think so, but these babies are almost weedless."

They tossed them into beds of old and emerging reeds and caught a northern pike every cast or two. It was good sport, but they threw them all back. They weren't as good to eat as the fish they already had. In the late afternoon they returned to the resort, cleaned their catch, and put limits on ice.

"Dad. Let's go to the Hilltop and get steaks for supper. What do you say?"

"OK Max. On one condition. Leave the cell phone behind. I want to talk."

"No problem. All incoming messages will be saved. I can get them later."

The weather cleared. They walked in bright sunshine to the restaurant and took seats by a picture window ready for a full view of a kind of sunset Blackduck was famous for. They ate full meals with big steaks and a couple of glasses of beer each.

"Max, you say that your office is where your phone and computer are."

"Yeah. That's the case for many people my age."

"Then, almost all of your time, you are at your office. You even prioritize calls with sound effects, like the bugle call for your boss, so you know who is important, who to interrupt, who to answer and who to put on hold. I notice that when we fish, the phone takes priority. Is that true when you're home, too?"

"I get a few complaints along those lines. Yes. But Dad, you don't understand. Most young people are in the same circumstances. Modern technology makes it so easy to communicate everywhere. It's just expected in today's workplace."

"This new stuff is wonderful, but it can create a mind-trap. It seems to have you chained to your job. Did you know that my dedication to work was one of the issues between me and your mother?"

"You mean like, 'Why are you never home. All the other fathers in the neighborhood are home by five, and they hardly travel. You leave me home alone to take care of the children.' Yeah, I remember that."

"Max, it would be tragic if your job would cause your marriage to break up."

"Oh, I don't think that will happen. Marge understands what business people have to go through these days."

"Remember when we came here the first time? I left those folders back in Minneapolis, and I had no phone, no way to get involved in work. Being alone with you for a few days freed my mind from work. I got a new perspective on what was important. I am hoping that you could unplug temporarily here on Blackduck and find the same kind of relief. Do I sound preachy?"

"Yeah," said Max. "But that's okay. I know you mean well."

"Are you willing to try something?"

"Sure, Dad. Almost anything."

"When we get back to the cabin, call home if you want. But then close down for business. Put the cell phone and computer away. Let's play cribbage. I brought a board. Or just bull shit. Talk about old times. Let's finalize plans for the reunion in Big Sky with your and your sisters' families. Let's give each other priority tonight and all day Sunday. How about fishing for crappies? Or going to Blackduck Island to spy on eagles? Or going around the shore to see how many species of ducks you remember from our long-ago visits. When we start back on Monday, I'll drive, and you can have your phone back. You'll have to go to work."

"I'll give it a try," said Max.

That evening and the next day, father and son spent uninterrupted time together. After they said goodbyes to Tim and Carolyn on Monday morning, John drove, and Max grabbed his cell phone and went back to work.

Back at the retirement home John got out, and they hugged. "Thanks, Max. I had a ball."

"Me, too, Dad. I feel more relaxed than I have for a long time. I'll try to find more occasions to unplug the phone and get away from my job."

Fishing in Pimushe

i

"PIMUSHE! PIMUSHE!? I DIDN'T know there were walleyes in Pimushe." Mr. Eon Keeper, the motel owner, kept staring at the twelve walleyes laid out on the cleaning table at the Mallard Motel in Blackduck, Minnesota one afternoon in late June. The cleaning shack was set back a respectable thirty feet from motel rooms. From the table and gut bucket sitting by its side sprung an unpleasant, but familiar, odor mingled with the smoke from a cigarette dangling from the Eon's lips.

The instant he had entered the shack he cried, "Wherdayagettum?"

Mike D. had replied, "Pimushe."

A puzzled look hung on the owner's brow. Pimushe was a shallow muddy lake, and even in good years, supplied limited catches of pan fish and bass, and occasionally a few small, newly stocked walleyes. In bad years, a few bullheads and a sunfish would be a good day's catch. "Where abouts did you get 'em in Pimushe?"

et al.

Neither Mike looked up from the filleting process, but Mike D. responded, "On the mid-lake structures."

This answer did not resolve the mystery, for Eon knew there weren't any mid-lake structures in Pimushe. Maybe one mud bottom could have been a little higher than a neighbor, but that wouldn't qualify as a "mid-lake structure." He politely asked the Mikes to step back from the table, so he could take a picture of the fish. Afterwards, he stood awkwardly by the door staring at the fish table. Several times his mouth formed to ask a question but couldn't get it out. He left the dim light of the cleaning shack and went to the office.

ii

"BROOKE, THOSE TWO GUYS from Minneapolis came in with a nice stringer of walleyes. Said they caught them in Pimushe. Got a photo here."

"Glad someone caught something." Brooke looked up from her ledger. "Fishing has been pretty awful, and we are near the end of the good crowds this season. Won't really pick up again until those two weeks in November for deer season."

Eon asked, "How are we going to get some cash to repair the showers? One more season without replacing the hot water pipes and there won't even be a pee stream through them. We're already getting complaints. And we just have to resurface the parking areas this year, or it will cost even more next year to completely repave 'em."

"If we get some good crowds the next few weeks, we will get by. I'll put a picture of that walleye catch on our website. That should bring in a few more customers," said Brooke.

"We need some good luck," said Eon. "But I really doubt those guys caught the fish in Pimushe."

"Pimushe's where they said they caught 'em. That's good enough for me."

⁝⁝⁝

THE TWO MIKES FINISHED cleaning, bagging, and icing the fish, and then headed to the motel room for some cold beer. They quickly polished off the first cans without saying a word and then popped open two more.

"Pimushe, huh? What made you think of that?" said Mike K. He snorted out a laugh.

"First lake that came to my head," said Mike D. Then he had a giggling fit. When he caught his breath, he continued, "Couldn't hardly tell them where Carl told us to fish. Promised him not to tell. He's been good to us."

"He sure knows this area," said Mike K.

et al.

"Well, he should. He's a guide. I'm glad we hired him a couple of times. It has sure paid off. With his advice we always catch more and larger fish than anyone else." Mike D. took another drag from the can.

"Well, Carl has benefited from our feedback to him, too." Mike K. added.

"Yep," agreed the other Mike. "We scratch his back and he scratches ours."

"If we'd told Eon the right lake, tomorrow twenty boats would follow us around and spoil our fishing," said Mike K.

"We wouldn't be able to land a fish without being spotted, and boats would be so close we would get our lines tangled with theirs. It would ruin the fishing. This way we should continue to have good fishing," said Mike D.

"Why do you think we always catch more than anyone? Is it just because we know Carl," asked Mike K.

"That's one reason. Another is our better equipment. That damned side-scanning sonar shows any fish within 100 feet of either side of the boat. No use in fishing where they're not."

"Do you feel bad about not telling the truth about where we caught the fish?" asked Mike K.

"Hell no. It's the kind of white lie every fisherman uses. Eon should know all about that custom. Besides, no one got hurt, right?"

"I guess not," Mike K. said.

iv

JOHN GOODMAN AND HIS boy, John Jr. checked in Friday night at the motel. "Just staying one night," he said to Brooke. "Saw your website and thought this would be a chance for my boy to catch his first walleye. I can only be away for one night."

"You can try Pimushe. As you saw on the web, some nice walleyes came out of there last week. Boat rentals are available, or do you have your own boat?" asked Brooke.

"Got my own. It ain't much, but it floats and gets me from here to there."

The Goodmans unpacked their few belongings in the motel room that had two twin beds and a bathroom with a shower — no frills. The nine-year-old Goodman said, "I don't know if I can sleep. I really want to catch a walleye like all my buddies."

"Tell you what, Son. If we have good luck tomorrow, you can choose two of your friends to come back here to go fishing with us. Deal?"

"Deal, Dad."

et al.

The next morning, they headed out to Pimushe using the map provided by the county tourism board. It was a good thing they had their own boat because all available boats were already rented. Father and son fished all day with different baits - minnows, leeches, night crawlers, and plugs. They fished with jigs and Lindy rigs. They fished deep, medium depth, and shallow, both fast and slow. They fished all day, taking time out only to eat the sandwiches Mrs. Goodman had packed for them. At the end of the day they had two rock bass, one bullhead, and a large-mouthed bass. No walleyes.

"This has been terrible fishing, Son. Sorry," said Mr. Goodman.

"That's alright, Dad. We tried. At least we got to spend some time together. You have been so busy lately." But the younger fisherman hung his head and fell silent on the trip back to the motel.

"We will have to find a different place to fish if we come up here with your buddies. This place is a bust," said John Senior.

𝑣

HOT WEATHER SET IN and fishing completely shut down in the Blackduck area. "Might as well turn off the vacancy sign. No one's gonna stop tonight," said Brooke.

"Agreed. It's going to be slim pickings until fall when we'll get a few duck hunters," said Eon. "And the best hope after that is a few deer hunters and fall fishermen."

"I made an appointment with the bank for us tomorrow morning at 10:00," said Brooke. "If we get that improvement loan, we can at least fix the hot water pipes and blacktop the parking lot. People won't stay here if we don't."

"They should give us a loan. We've banked there for over twenty years."

"Just to play it safe, I made sure our business looks good on the balance sheet, just a little better than it really is," said Brooke.

"Brooke, you didn't cook the books, did you?" asked Eon.

"Not exactly cooked, just warmed 'em up a little," she said.

vi

FIFTY-SIX-YEAR-OLD VICE PRESIDENT, John Greene, of the Blackduck Wells Fargo Bank was meeting with the loan committee in the conference room of the small brick building on Main Street. John was worried. The branch needed more business, and the aging officer couldn't afford to lose his position. He'd never find another.

A short stack of loan applications lay on the conference table, and the committee was reviewing them one-by-one. "The next one is from the Keeper's Motel. They want to fix the place up a bit," said John.

"It damned well needs fixing up," remarked Bill M. Back, the only attorney in town. "It's a wonder someone hasn't stepped in a hole in that parking lot and broke a leg."

"Parking lot resurfacing is one of the repairs they list in the application," said John.

"I'm a little concerned that the improvements are coming too late," said Penny Sicher, the teller and an assistant to the vice president. "I haven't seen a lot of activity there this year, even in the spring. The parking lot hasn't had two cars at once in the past month. Do you think we could be putting a bad loan on our books?"

"Well, no loan is without risk," said John. "The Keepers aren't alone with business troubles. The poor fishing has been really tough on local resorts unless they can advise people where and how to fish."

"We could deny the loan," said Bill.

"Y'know, Bill, we have Blackduck's only bank. If we don't make loans, Wells Fargo could shut down our branch," said the vice president.

"And if the loans are bad?" asked Penny.

"They will shut us down even quicker," said John. "Look, I think we should give the Keepers their loan. They've been with us a long time, and they're honest folks. They'll make the required payments."

He moved the application to the 'approved pile' for Penny to award.

vii

"WHERE SHOULD WE GO fishing this year?" said Mike K. "Maybe back to Blackduck? Several years ago, we had good luck in that area."

"No way. Fishing has always been tough in that region, and Carl has moved. Now there aren't any experts for us to tap," said Mike D.

"Coming home from duck hunting last fall I noticed that the Mallard Motel was closed," said Mike K.

"I stopped in town last fall myself," said Mike D. "Blackduck doesn't even have a bank anymore."

"Saw an advertisement for Whipolt Resort on Leech. They had pictures of long stringers of walleyes held by their patrons," said Mike K.

Mike D. grinned. "No telling where the fish were caught."

His Last Fly-in

Day 1

WITH A BLACK WALKING pole firmly in each hand, Carl tottered toward the deHavilland Twin Otter waiting at the dock. His hooded sweatshirt and jeans hung loosely on his spare, ninety-year-old frame, and the 2013 Showalter cap sat over his thinning gray hair, shielding his bloodshot, impaired eyes from the morning sun.

"How many years will this make, Carl?" said young Eddie, fiftyish, well-built, six foot four, with a pock-marked and deeply tanned face, in blue jeans and a flannel shirt. He spoke fast with a clipped Ontario accent. Ed Showalter, his father, had retired four years ago leaving Eddie to run the wilderness fly-in business consisting of three float planes and seven fishing camps.

"This one makes twenty-nine," Carl said slowly and softly, carefully articulating his words. "The family insists this is my last. My son-in-law, Mike, is along on the trip. Otherwise they wouldn't have wanted me to come this time."

Carl Nomura recalled his first trip to Carroll Lake when he was in his early sixties. Five acquaintances from Honeywell and two from the Unitarian Church went with him. They have all died, all of them. He studied this current group assembled on the dock waiting to board the plane.

Jim Daughton had aged since forty years ago when Carl hired him into Honeywell. Jim was still almost six feet tall, but he had lost weight and his hair was snow white. Mike Daughton, his son, was a big man, six three and two hundred fifty pounds. Laura, Mike's petite pre-teen daughter wore practical fishing clothing, but all in color-coordinated pastels.

Mike Daughton, the organizer for the trip, said, "Well, I'm a Mike and we have two other Mikes in our party. I have a suggestion that could avoid confusion. Mike Kuethe can be called Slow Jerk. He got that nickname from a Native American friend who thought him slow to set the hook. Carl's son-in-law, Mike, can go by Captain Mike due to his many years as a ship's engineer. In years past I've been called Walleye Master. Not sure the nickname's that appropriate, but at least I'll come when called. That okay with the group?"

The group grunted and nodded up and down.

Carl said, "You know, I once had a friend with a wife named Marie, a daughter named Marie, and a dog named Marie. When asked how he got by at home, he said, "When I want someone, I call Marie, and then I send back the ones I don't want.""

"I'll bet that was one happy family," said Jim.

"I'll need a little help getting Carl into the plane when we board," said Captain Mike, a spare, wiry type, also donning a 2013 Showalter Cap.

"I volunteer," said Slow Jerk.

"Will you need help, Dave?" asked Walleye Master. Dave was Mike Daughton's father-in-law. He had been trampled by his farm bull only a few days ago and suffered cuts and bruises. His decision to come was last minute.

"Don't think I need help. But maybe someone could spot me on the way up."

Carl thought to himself that the spotter could have a dangerous task. Dave weighed two sixty.

"It's time to go." Eddie called to Carl's group on the dock, "Come on over to the plane and hop on. Part of your gear will have to go later in the Beaver, but all seven of you can go in this plane."

With strong men on each arm, Carl managed to climb the aluminum steps into the airplane. The others in his party followed. Laura got to ride in the copilot's seat.

Kaworu (Carl) Nomura was born June 22, 1922 in a boxcar in Montana, the son of migratory farm workers. His father died when he was six years old, and his mother moved to Los Angeles with Carl, his sister, and two brothers, where his mother opened a grocery store. At the start of World War II, the family was confined in an internment camp in Arizona with others of Japanese ancestry, and all their property was lost. Carl enlisted in the Army in 1943 and was thereby allowed to leave the camp. After the war he went to the University of Minnesota, the only school that would accept him with his Japanese heritage. Years and years later, he donated his entire reparations check to that school. Carl married a young nurse, Louise, who was also of Japanese descent. Together they raised four children, all of them college graduates with successful careers. He was happy with the way his family turned out.

Carl earned a PhD in physics and began a forty-year career at Honeywell where he was eventually promoted to Senior Vice President. Many credited him with converting Honeywell from a lagging technology company to a leader.

Eddie climbed atop the fuselage of the Otter and lowered himself into the cockpit through the top hatch, pulled it shut, and latched it. After the passengers strapped in seatbelts, he started the right engine. When it was roaring, he started the left engine. He pulled out into the Trout River and taxied toward the bigger water of Lac Seul, paying careful attention to the airplane's instrument panel in addition to all the pontoon settings. Out in Lac Seul he turned the airplane into the west wind and revved the engines, making the passengers glad for ear protection. The plane left the water, gaining altitude as it crossed the road to Ear Falls. The plane settled into a westward flight at some two thousand feet. Gentle vibrations in the cabin combined with throbbing engine noise had an almost hypnotizing effect as the plane flew past Red Lake and onto the sixty miles route over roadless territory to Carroll Lake.

It had been many years since Carl could see well enough to look out the window and see the ground clearly, but his mind recalled the endless landscape of green trees, black and brown rocky hills, and water, particularly the water. All of those lakes and rivers were interconnected in mysterious patterns. The mouths of some streams had brown and green vegetation spilling out for hundreds of feet into the deep blue lake water.

Carl mused about all those raindrops that made the lakes. They fell from the skies, each with a nirvana goal of reaching the Arctic Sea by going through Lake Winnipeg and Hudson's Bay. Almost none made it. They were vaporized prematurely back into the sky to await new assignments.

Carl thought of all the things he had done for the last time...like when he left Honeywell with nothing to do for the company the next day. How surprised he was to find how quickly the days filled with new assignments - talking to grandchildren, traveling, writing books, raising a garden, and playing cards. He remembered his last tennis game. He could only hobble around and just guessed where the ball was hit, aided by sound and blurred vision. He remembered the last time he saw his wife Louise, the day of that terrible car accident. God, how he missed her! They argued a lot. They used to refer to each other as 'My

et al.

Debate Opponent'. Well, how does that saying go? "There is a first time for everything." Well, there's a last time, too.

Carl wasn't a bit nervous with Eddie in the pilot's seat. Eddie had flown the route since he was sixteen and could easily fly it visually without GPS even if he could see the ground only occasionally. On this partly cloudy day the plane passed Hammerhead Lake and Donald ahead of that, and then the falls into Carroll. The plane turned lower over the camp and banked around down near the water, lightly rippled by a ten mile per hour breeze. Eddie manipulated the pontoon controls and came in for a perfectly smooth landing.

"Wow, Eddie" Mike Daughton said. "You shoulda been a bush pilot."

"Pretty good, eh?" responded Eddie. He slowed the plane's guide in toward the dock. The group leaving the camp was waiting there. He opened the hatch, climbed on the fuselage, jumped down, grabbed a rope, and tied up the airplane.

Carl's group got down the ladder one at a time to the dock, Carl coming last. With one strong man on each arm, he carefully descended. Captain Mike had Carl's two walking poles at the ready, and Carl made his way to the shore.

Pleasant and welcome pine and water smells at Carroll hadn't changed in all those years. Not so pleasant was the faint odor of fish offal from the cleaning table on a cliff overlooking the lake. Some smoke still rose from the smoldering fire pit where the previous residents had burned trash. Further beyond the cabin the outhouse leaked the faint smell of human waste.

A human chain unloaded things from the plane to shore one item at a time and then loaded the departing stuff into the plane. As the plane left with the departing group, Carl's group packed away their baggage, fishing gear, and groceries into the cabin. Carl wanted to help, but could only pack away his own belongings, including a contraption for urinating at night and several bottles of eye drops which had to be stored in the propane refrigerator.

The cabin was spacious for this neck of the woods. There were two bedrooms, one with three bunk beds and the other with three cots. Carl, Jim, and Dave got bottom bunks and Captain Mike took a top bunk. Three cots were claimed by Walleye Master, Laura, and Slow Jerk. The large kitchen had a propane stove, a sink with running water, and a large table for seating up to ten.

Carl remembered when jumping in the cold lake was the only way to bathe. Ed had built a hot water shower uphill from the outhouse. Nice addition.

After a quickie lunch, the group went fishing. Walleye Master, Jim, and Laura were in one boat, Dave and Slow Jerk in another, and Carl and Captain Mike in a third. Walleye Master's boat led the way to the mouth of Donald Lake Falls. It was a beautiful site. Water from Donald Lake cascaded noisily down the half mile and two hundred feet elevation drop the lake to Carroll. A strong current rippled five hundred feet into Carroll creating eddies around large boulders lying on the bottom.

The boats idled in quieter water of the bay. Each fisherman impaled a frozen minnow on a weighted jig and lowered it near the bottom. Almost at once fish bent spinning rods into sharp arcs. Walleyed pike were reeled in and netted. These beautiful golden bronze fish lived in a current, which made them especially strong, and they fought hard. "Keep fish between fifteen and seventeen inches," yelled Walleye Master. "They're the best eating. Throw the others back."

Carl caught a nice twenty-two-inch fish, and very reluctantly threw it back. People who haven't lived part of their life hungry wouldn't understand. Carl remembered eating green peppers three times a day when they were picking peppers, onions three times a day when harvesting onions, and so forth. He would never be really comfortable throwing back perfectly good food, but he went along. The three boats quickly caught enough fish for supper, Laura and Carl catching their shares.

Back at camp, Jim said, "Relax and get ready for supper. I'll take the fish." After Jim cleaned the fish, Slow Jerk and Captain Mike took the fish guts across the lake to a rock visible from the camp. Sea gulls gwakked and were first to get at the tasty treat, but three eagles quickly swooped in and took charge.

Mike Daughton cooked the fish, some in butter and lemon, and others with soy sauce and garlic. Side dishes were potato chips, lettuce salad, and oranges for dessert. Beer, more beer, and whiskey were the chief beverages for all but Laura, who drank pop. Dinner was over about 6:00 PM, so there was time to go fishing until 8:30 PM when the sun began to set, and the mosquitoes began to rise. Carl was tired and decided to stay home and rest.

To Carl fishing was meant to be a social event. Boat talk, dinner talk, and after dinner talk were what he valued most. He targeted each member of the party for intense conversations about themselves and the meaning of life. He was also interested in observing how the group worked together. With his visual and hearing impairments, boat talk was usually difficult. His best time for socializing was when everyone came back from fishing in the evening. He could adjust his hearing aids just so and made sure he sat in a good light. In the meantime, until they returned, he read a book on the cello.

The first evening after fishing Laura's father played an iPod recording of Laura performing Debussy's *Clare de Lune* at a piano recital. Everyone at the table clapped, and Laura, a pretty brown-haired girl, blushed.

Slow Jerk said, "Laura, show them your sketch book. They are really good."

et al.

The group passed around Laura's pencil drawings. "It's really not much," said Laura.

"Buy her a water color set," suggested Captain Mike.

"I'm really not interested in color at this time—just black and white," said Laura.

"Can a grandfather put in his two cents," piped up Jim. "Laura won the English prize last year at her school, and her first poem is about to be published in a book."

"Mike, what are you going to do about this?" Carl asked her father. "You have a big responsibility here."

"Don't know what to say," said Walleye Master. "I guess we'll give her the chance to develop any way she wants and can. She'll be twelve next month and she goes to a great private school. We'll encourage her in every way."

"Laura, would you give me your email address?" asked Carl. They exchanged email addresses. Carl would make sure that Mike would help her develop her talents.

Day 2

FOR THE REMAINDER OF the stay at Carroll, every morning Jim arose at least half an hour earlier than anyone else to prepare coffee and a big breakfast by 6:00 AM. He made toast over the propane burner, fried bacon or sausages in a big frying pan, and sometimes fried potatoes. Jim personalized breakfasts as people got to the table using a different frying pan, offering eggs cooked any way or pancakes. Cold cereal, milk, apples, and oranges were set in the middle of the table along with plastic ware, paper plates, and paper towels for napkins.

As soon as the kitchen was cleaned up, everyone went fishing. The fish were biting, as usual, and a few were kept, cleaned, and refrigerated. Lunch was eaten ad hoc and was followed by more fishing. In the late afternoon enough fish were cleaned and cooked for each person to have four good-sized fillets. Slow Jerk coated walleye fillets with Shore Lunch and cooked them in oil on the outside propane burner. Baked potatoes and coleslaw filled out the meal with cookies for dessert. After supper cleanup, another round of fishing ensued. Carl and Dave didn't go fishing with the others.

"Why aren't you going fishing?" asked Carl.

"Carl, I'm pretty stiff and sore. I got hurt by a bull a few days ago. I wasn't even sure I could come on this trip." Dave showed Carl some of his many bruises and abrasions.

"How did it happen?"

"We were trying to herd the bull into a truck, and I thought I could turn him by standing in front of him. He didn't like that and ran right through me.

"Farming has risks, doesn't it?"

et al.

"Yep. Fortunately, my full time job is a real estate broker. I work with foreclosed properties," said Dave.

"Let me ask you a question. What was Laura's mother like when she was Laura's age?"

"Kim was a good athlete, horse lover, good student. She got a college scholarship in track and a degree in communications. I was very proud of her. Still am."

"Any other children?"

"Yep. A daughter and a son. Both married and both with kids. I'm a grandfather eight times. How about your children, Carl?"

"I have four and everything is well with them. As my mother used to say 'No one is in jail. Isn't that wonderful?' All got degrees, two of them PhD's. All the grandchildren are doing well. Two of my granddaughters came here when they were Laura's age."

Carl read his cello book and Dave did some paperwork involved in selling foreclosed properties until the fishing boats pulled in. The whole crew sat around the table, the three Mikes and Jim drinking scotch, Carl drinking beer, and Laura drinking soda.

"I want to make teriyaki walleye tomorrow for supper," said Carl. "And I would like to make fish soup for lunch."

"How many fish do you want?" asked Mike.

"Five for the soup and ten for the teriyaki."

"We'll have 'em for you by mid-morning," said Walleye Master.

Day 3

AFTER BREAKFAST THE NEXT morning, Carl located the ingredients for fish soup and teriyaki walleye - onions, garlic, soy sauce, sweet wine, ramen noodles, celery, and rice vinegar. He proceeded to peel and chop and fill various bowls in preparation for cooking. He put two pounds of rice in a big kettle of boiling water, making quite a bit more rice that was needed. Because of his bad eyesight he made a big mess, but he knew Captain Mike and others would help clean it up. He wanted badly to contribute, and cooking was one of the only ways he could help. The boats came back at mid-morning as promised, and the soup was ready for adding the five walleyes, which needed only a few minutes of cooking. The soup was the main dish for lunch.

"You've outdone yourself, Carl," chorused the group. "Way to go."

"We have more rice than we need. Jim, could you save a cup of bacon grease tomorrow morning, so I can make fried rice?"

"Sure, Carl. No problem"

"The marinade for teriyaki walleye is in this bowl," said Carl.

Mike Daughton added the ten walleyes into the bowl to marinate until supper time, and the crew cleaned up. Cooked rice was tracked around the stove, and cleanup took some special effort. At supper time Mike Daughton cooked the marinated walleyes on the outside propane grill. The party was unanimous in proclaiming that dish the best ever and toasted Carl. He was able to gloat a bit. Jim also made spaghetti with meat sauce to round out the meal.

After the evening fishing trip, the group once again sat around the big table. Laura asked to be excused and went to bed.

Jim asked, "Carl, you going to write any more books?"

"No, I'm through writing books. *Sleeping on Potatoes* is still selling, but slowly. My management book was translated into Japanese and is selling well in Japan. Jim, do you remember Susumo Koyami? He was the translator."

"Sure I remember him. He was a Toshiba representative at Honeywell and worked in my group. Twice when I made trips to Japan, he and his wife took time from their busy schedules to take care of me in Tokyo. Once a friend, always a friend. They really take care of you. What has happened to him?"

"He left the board of Toshiba and became the president of a start-up. Haven't heard from him for a few months."

"How is your last book doing, Carl?" asked Jim.

"My book on solving Sudoku puzzles? I wrote it because another writer claimed his puzzles weren't solvable by any method. I wrote him showing how easily his puzzles were solved by my technique, but he never returned my letter. Writing books is a lot of work for small rewards. I'm going to take up the cello. I'm reading this book to prepare."

"Carl," said Captain Mike, "your cello should arrive about the time we get back home."

"I'm looking forward to that," said Carl. "I wish I could play a duet some day with Laura."

"What else is going on with you, Carl?" asked Jim.

"I'm being interviewed by the newspaper about the major decisions I've made in my life."

"Carl, do you have to tell about bad decisions as well as good ones?" asked Jim. "Or did you make any bad ones?"

"Many, but the two I regret most were turning down a job with William Schottky, an inventor of the transistor, when he left Bell Labs to form a company. And then not working with Bob Noyce when he formed Intel. I could have been really rich. I worked for Honeywell, instead."

"You did pretty well, anyway, Carl," said Jim.

"One of my great disappointments was when Ed Spencer made Tom Kurtson my manager. He was a real asshole. Don't you agree, Jim?"

"He was a pretty tough customer, all right." But you know he taught me an important principle."

et al.

"What was that?"

"In scheduling and budgeting, sometimes things get a little behind and others a little ahead. Some things cost more than estimated and some less. In the end, things turn out about on-plan. Tom called this LOCFU, the Law Of Compensating Fuck-Ups." The men around the table laughed. They hoped Laura hadn't heard the F-bomb in the bedroom.

Day 4

THE NEXT MORNING, JIM set aside a cup of bacon grease for Carl. A typical huge breakfast was served as campers arrived and got to the table. There were a few teriyaki walleye fillets left over, and Slow Jerk ate them cold. Walleye Master packed three lunches for Laura, Jim, and himself. They were to hike to Donald Lake for fishing lake trout and wouldn't be back until late afternoon. Dave and Captain Mike in one boat, and Slow Jerk and Carl in another went to Donald Falls and fished leisurely in the deeper, quiet water. Without a motor running and no wind, Carl could even hear well enough to carry on a conversation with Slow Jerk.

"Slow Jerk, how did you get to know Walleye Master?"

"We both worked in finance for Brown Communications. We got to talking one day and found we both liked fishing. I had lost my dad, my long-term fishing pal. I think Walleye Master had some sympathy for me, and he invited me fishing a couple of times. It worked out well, and we fish together a lot."

"Where do you fish?" asked Carl.

"Lots a places. Couple of times a year in South Dakota, in and around Black Duck Lake in Minnesota. Red Lake. Jim goes usually goes with us."

"Mike and Jim seem to enjoy fishing together. Do you think Mike thinks about the loss of your father when he invites Jim," asked Carl.

"I think there's something to that," said Slow Jerk.

"How do you get away to fish so often, Mike?"

"My wife and I don't have kids, and she has her own interests when I fish. It works out okay."

The two boats fished until they had limits of good fish to freeze and take home. They returned to the cabin. Slow Jerk and Captain Mike cleaned the fish and stored them in the freezer. Carl made about a gallon of fried rice with celery, onions, garlic, lots of soy sauce, and of course the cup of bacon grease. They ate fried rice and some leftovers for lunch and then went fishing nearby at Hager's Falls, catching and releasing fish.

Walleye Master, Jim, and Laura came back from Donald with three lake trout. Jim cleaned them, put two in the freezer to take home and left one out for supper. The freezer held possession limits of walleyes, so no more fish could be kept.

It was time for the group's customary bratwurst and sauerkraut supper. Mike marinated the bratwurst in beer and Jim cooked the brats on the grill. He also toasted the buns. Mike added Canadian bacon and onions to the sauerkraut and served it in a small kettle. A large stainless steel pan held lettuce with tomatoes, onions, and cucumbers. Three bottles of prepared dressings sat by the pan. Grilled lake trout was an appetizer and Carl's fried rice rounded out the meal.

"What should we do after supper?" asked Mike.

"Let's go to the narrows," suggested Slow Jerk.

"Great idea," said Carl. "I haven't been there for years."

So it was that after cleanup the group piled into three boats and traveled the length of the lake thirty miles to the point where all the lake flowed westward to Manitoba and formed a tributary to the Winnipeg River. They fished a little, not very seriously, and released all they caught. As the sun got lower, they all headed back to the Carroll dock.

The group sat around drinking and talking after supper. Laura spoke up. "You've known my grandpa a long time. What was he like when he worked for you?"

"You know, Laura, your grandfather was a smart man," said Carl. "And he was unusual in this respect. I could give him an assignment at quitting time, and the next morning he was likely to have it done. He flattened any barrier in the way of a goal. That trait bothered some people. For example, the Indian fishing guide at Cochrane Lake called him 'that hyper son-of-a-bitch'. He could be very tough at work. Your father, Mike, seems a little hyper, too, but he comes across a little less intense."

"He's a good dad, alright. But I wish we could sleep in some morning instead of fishing all the time."

"I see intensity when we fish," said Slow Jerk will a grin. "He isn't all that laid-back."

"I want to tell everyone that Carl was a terrific boss," said Jim. He always listened to me (and everyone else) and had the complete trust of management in Honeywell. He had a loyal following from the bottom to the top of the organization, including the president.

"What became of the jump-rope company, Carl?" asked Mike Daughton

"Oh, you remember that? It was really in bad shape when I went on the board after I retired from Honeywell. It was a small local company that employed the unemployable—the physically, emotionally, or mentally handicapped, ex-cons, the homeless. They made jump-ropes and baked bread and tried to sell those and other goods at competitive prices. We turned them around. It is now a $100M company making almost $10M per year."

et al.

"What turned them around?" asked Dave.

"The most significant factor was hiring the right person to run it. We fired the president and hired a real winner. He was the one who actually turned it around, but the board deserved credit for seeing what was wrong and getting the right person in charge."

Day 5

AFTER A HEARTY BREAKFAST, the last full day in camp was spent part fishing and part getting ready to leave. No additional fish could be kept without exceeding limits, so there could be no more fish for lunch and supper. Mike grilled hamburgers and heated a large pot of canned baked beans for lunch. Jim grilled steak and onions and made a large lettuce salad for supper. Slow Jerk and Mike Daughton worked at putting away fishing gear and getting the boats in order for the next crew coming in. Between times everyone made short fishing excursions near camp, catching and releasing more walleyes in a couple of hours than most Minnesota fishermen catch in an entire season. After supper, most of the remaining beer and scotch was consumed, and once again all sat around the kitchen table.

"Carl, how does this trip compare with your other trips to Carroll Lake?" asked Dave.

"There are a few differences, mostly positive. The camp is a lot more modern than it was twenty-nine years ago. Propane lights give off a lot more light than the old Coleman lanterns. You can get a warm shower. The cabin is much larger. The fishing is not quite as good if my memory serves me right. But there are many things the same. The lake, the trees, the smells—they are wonderful. And the comradery was special. This trip has been great. I've really enjoyed the time we spent together.

"What is memorable about this trip, Carl?" asked Captain Mike.

"Well, it's the people and how they function together. Captain Mike, you are my son-in-law, so knew you pretty well before we came. Thanks for your help. I'm also glad I met Slow Jerk and Dave, both great company. But the Daughtons are special to me. Jim worked for me for fifteen years and has been a friend for forty. Jim wouldn't be here at Carroll if I hadn't convinced him to come."

"That's for sure, Carl. And thanks for a lot of other things you've done for me over our long friendship," said Jim.

"Except for my son-in-law, the rest of you all are here indirectly as a result of my friendship with Jim here, and then with Mike. I remember little Mike as a baby and then a boy and now a man. And now here's Laura. It's really interesting to see three generations here at Carroll and see how each is developing. It makes me feel this Carroll trip will go on and on, and I've had a part in keeping it going."

"My son James II will come here in two years, too," said Mike.

et al.

"If this is to be your last trip here, Carl, what will take its place for you?" asked Slow Jerk.

"For sure I will study the cello. I will spend time with my children and grandchildren, and if lucky, maybe with great-grandchildren. I won't worry too much about the future. Some new challenges will come up to make life interesting. They always have."

The group gave a toast to a successful trip and retired to bed.

Going Home

Five days at Carroll Lake had by all too quickly, and it was time to clean the cabin for the next group. Jim burned the garbage starting with a large wood fire. That fire burned long and hot enough to dry out wet garbage and then burn it. A head of cabbage finally burned after being in the fire an hour. Plastic was burned, too, even if environmentalists wouldn't approve. There was a trade-off between the expense of flying out a big load of plastic bottles and a small amount of air pollution. Slow Jerk and Walleye Master had the boats cleaned and gassed for the next arrivals.

Carl helped sweep part of the cabin. Slow Jerk mopped the floor and finished just before the Otter landed. The arriving group got off the plane and Carl's party boarded. The Otter took off from Carroll Lake, climbed skyward, and returned to the mouth of Lac Seul at Trout River. Carl slept through the return trip. Once again Eddy made a perfect landing and saw to it the group and their baggage disembarked.

Others in the group enthused in the office about next year, but Carl knew this was his last trip to Carroll Lake. He had accomplished what he set out to do. Pleasant memories of Carroll were indelibly stored in his mind. Carl would work on his cello and other new assignments as they came up.

Paxton

IN EARLY APRIL OF 1996, Russ piloted a Jeep that pulled a boat west along Interstate 90 in South Dakota. Big Z, Russ's father, sat in the copilot's seat, and my son Mike and I rode in back. The sunny day, the hum of snow tires, and the monotonous flat terrain combined to make the passengers drowsy. Big Z broke the tedium. "Hope we know what we're getting into, staying on an Indian reservation."

Russ said, "Dad, the proper name is now Native American."

Mike piped in, "Raleigh, says not to worry about the locals, and Lake Sharpe is a fisherman's paradise compared to Lake Francis Case."

I remarked, "Raleigh knows his stuff about fishing. We've seen enough of that when we fished with him on Francis Case. But getting held up or mugged wouldn't be worth it."

"Dad, you worry too much," Mike said. "I've read up on the area. The Lower Brule Tribe is progressive. They produce all the popcorn for the National Basketball Association. A South Dakota sports magazine said the motel at the Golden Buffalo Casino is friendly and safe. You'll see. It's not as bad as some other Native American towns."

We turned off of I 90 at Chamberlin and traveled on a secondary road along the east shoreline of Lake Francis Case on our route to Lake Sharpe. Our quartet reminisced about fishing spots we passed. "There're the columns," said Russ. A virtual forest of dead tree trunks rose out of the water ten feet and marked the area where we caught many walleyes but lost many lead jigs on subsurface tree limbs.

"We'd better stop off in Fort Thomson for gas and minnows," said Mike. "Raleigh said neither are available in Lower Brule."

Russ pulled into Lynn's Dakotamart in the town of 1300 residents, mostly Native Americans, and parked at one of the six gas pumps. "I'll do the gas," I said. My companions went inside to buy minnows and a few groceries.

As I started to fuel the Jeep, a Native American staggered up. He wore a red and black flannel shirt, blue jeans, and a cowboy hat atop black hair that fell in two shoulder-length braids. He was smoking a cigarette. "Hey, you from Minnesota?"

"Yes, I am."

"Do you really have 10,000 lakes like it says on the license plate?"

"Yes, maybe even a few more."

"Then why the fuck don't you fish in one of them?" he asked

I tried not to be flustered. "Why, the season isn't open in Minnesota," I said.

He continued to stare at me. I was very nervous with a burning cigarette next to flowing gasoline. My visitor reeked of alcohol and rocked unsteadily. I replaced the gas hose and walked quickly toward the store. My new friend tried to follow, but I lost him somewhere in the small crowd of farmers gathered at the only store selling groceries for forty miles.

The four of us got back in the vehicle. "Let's get to hell out of here," I said. "The locals don't seem all that friendly." I related my encounter.

"It's to be expected here," said Mike. "The Crow Creek Tribe has big problems according to Raleigh. Half the men are unemployed, and drugs and alcohol are everywhere. There's also a lot of anger here. But don't assume that all Native Americans are like the one you met."

Russ said, "Are you some kind of area expert, Mike?"

"Well, I listened to Raleigh and read a lot," he said.

We drove west across the Big Bend Dam. Lake Francis Case lay downstream and stretched 107 miles to the Fort Randall Dam. Lake Sharpe stretched 70 miles upstream to Pierre. Water from the power dam's turbines roared with fury out from the bottom of the dam into Lake Francis Case.

"In 1963, when the Big Bend Dam was completed, the original town of Lower Brule went underwater along with the rich Missouri River bottomland the tribe had farmed," Mike said. "The tribe sued the federal government and won reparations."

"Is the tribe still upset with palefaces?" I asked.

"Don't know," said Mike. "I hope not."

We drove along the west shore of Lake Sharpe for ten miles to Lower Brule, a town of about 1000 residents living in 300 small houses. We stopped at Sitting Bull Avenue at the outskirts.

"What time is it?" Russ asked.

"It's only 2:30. Why don't we go fishing?" Mike asked.

"Let's do it," said Russ. "I have a map that will get us to Iron Nation Bay. Raleigh said that was a good spot, didn't he?"

"That's right," said Mike.

THE PARKING LOT AT Iron Nation Bay was empty. A South Dakota fish and game sign was riddled with bullet holes. We boarded Russ's 17-foot fishing boat and shoved off onto Lake Sharp with Russ in the captain's seat.

There was a light breeze, and ripples in the water sparkled in the bright sunlight. The air smelled fresh and clean. Four rods were soon rigged. We expected good luck in the bay, but after a couple of hours we hadn't had a bite. "Why did we come all this way for this kind of fishing?" complained Big Z.

We trailered the boat and went back to the motel next to the Golden Buffalo Casino. A historical marker announced this was the site of the treaty signing of 1878 ceding these lands to the Lower Brule Tribe of Chief Iron Nation. The sign was decorated with twenty-three bullet holes and dents.

A white lady at the motel window in the casino found our reservation on her computer. We checked into two rooms, one for Big Z and his son and the other for Mike and me. After unloading our baggage from the Jeep, still grumbling about the poor fishing, Big Z headed to the casino for a pre-dinner drink. Mike, Russ, and I stretched out in our rooms for a little rest before heading for supper in the restaurant.

A wave of cigarette smoke met us as we entered the Golden Buffalo Casino. We walked by rows of one-armed bandits with zombie gamblers sitting by them. Bells and buzzers sounded a loud cacophony. Big Z was waiting for us at a table for four in the casino restaurant. Thankfully, smoking was not allowed there.

We were just seated when a stocky Native American walked up and straddled a chair next to our table. Invading Big Z's personal space by several inches, he addressed him nose-to-nose in a gravely smoker's voice. "Launch from Iron Nation. Go to the channel and you'll find two stumps, like this." He used his forefingers to represent the stumps. "Tie a rope to the left one, not the right one, and then go out to deep water stringing out the rope from the stump, and anchor. Come back to water thirty-eight to forty-one feet deep, and tie off the ropes to the boat, both from the anchor and from the stump. Fish stationary with a minnow about this far from the bottom." He used a thumb and forefinger about half an inch apart to show how far. "Be patient. If they don't bite right away, then bullshit a while, have a beer. They'll bite." With that he walked back through the restaurant door, leaving so suddenly we couldn't ask him a question.

"Who the hell was that character?" I asked my three companions.

"Just a local gone a little haywire," said Russ.

We looked around the room at the Native Americans eating dinner and the Native American wait staff. Could any of them be crazy, too?

All four of us ordered $4.95 prime rib dinners. We finished a supper that included salad from a giant bar and ice cream and then turned in back in our rooms.

Before the sun came up, we ate breakfast from the refrigerator and packed a lunch. We drove back to Iron Nation. On our way we saw a flock of turkeys, four whitetail deer, and two mule deer. Walking from the Jeep to the dock, we were awed by the rosy sunrise reflecting off Lake Shape in the east. While launching our boat, we heard cock pheasants crowing and coyote pups yelping.

We fished in the bay until late morning using our tried-and-true techniques without catching anything, and we almost despaired. "What the hell, we might as well try what that crazy Native American suggested," said Russ. It was his boat, so the rest of us, Big Z, Mike, and I, agreed.

We motored out into the channel and were bewildered by the hundreds of tree stumps protruding above water. But there were two that looked like the forefingers of that stranger, and we tied a rope to the left one, not the right one. Stringing the rope behind the boat, we went to deep water, and threw out the anchor, and let the anchor rope run as we went back toward the stump. At a depth of forty-one feet, we tied off both the anchor rope and the rope from the stump. We put minnows onto lead-head jigs, lowered them just off the bottom. Almost at once Mike yelled, "Fish On!" as his rod bowed toward the water.

"Me, too!" said Russ.

"A triple!" said Big Z.

"The crazy Local was trying to help us," I said.

We couldn't land the nice-sized walleyes fast enough to use our only landing net, and we had to hoist our catches out of the water and into the boat. For the next half-hour, the action was fast and furious, the best fishing ever. When we each had our four-fish limit, we headed to the landing and then to the cleaning table in the parking lot.

Back at the motel we set up a Coleman stove out of the wind. We fried four of the fish along with some potatoes and ate an appetite-sized 'shore dinner'. We kicked back, each of us with a can of beer.

"Isn't this place beautiful?" said Mike.

"It really has great scenery," I said. "Orange, black, and red cliffs, looking to be one hundred feet high, and broad green and brown plains bordering the lake."

"Don't go getting mushy on us," said Russ.

"I can't believe the wild life here," said Mike. "Raleigh was right."

"So far, so good. But are the tribe members really okay?" I asked. "We may yet hear from the bad guys."

Four contented fishermen, we drank beer in our rooms until suppertime. As we walked to the casino for supper, our Native American fishing advisor stood just inside the door. We introduced ourselves.

"Hi, I'm Paxton," he said. He was five eleven with reddish brown skin. Three of his top front teeth were missing as were two on the bottom. His medium length hair was gray. His nose was fairly large, but flattened, like the Indian's picture on the cheap, red, paper tablets we bought as young school children. Paxton was smoking a cigarette.

"Thank you, Paxton, for putting us on a great fishing spot. Won't you join us for supper?" asked Russ.

"OK," he grunted.

With five of us seated, we all ordered the prime rib special except for Paxton, who ordered 'the usual' from our Native American waitress. The regular turned out to be hamburger steak with American fries, cooked really crisp, and a Coke. Paxton stayed at the table when the rest of us went to the salad bar. Over dinner we had a chance to talk.

"Where are you guys from?" asked Paxton.

"All from Minnesota," said Russ.

"Paxton, were you born on the Lower Brule Reservation? I asked."

"No, I was born on the Pine Ridge Reservation out by Rapid City. Dad and I worked on I 90 construction near Chamberlin, and I decided to live in Lower Brule. It was so much better than that hellhole at Pine Ridge, which is almost as bad as that sorry bunch around Fort Thompson. As a full-blooded Sioux, I applied for Lower Brule tribal membership. After a few years, I was accepted."

et al.

Paxton continued. "I married Carline, a white woman. We met in Chamberlain. She now teaches part time at Head Start here in Lower Brule. We have three children, all out on their own and doing well. Big Z has met my daughter."

"I have?" asked Biz Z.

"Yeah, she's the bartender."

Then it clicked in. Big Z had complained to the bartender the evening before about poor fishing. She was Paxton's daughter. She must have told Paxton we were an unhappy bunch and asked him to help us.

"One of our sons is adopted," said Paxton.

"A family member?" asked Russ.

"Nope. Wife and I went to Mass and the priest announced a baby boy was left on the church steps. No one knew who left him. We took him home, got attached to him, and adopted him. We treated him the same as our two natural children. He's doing really well since he finished high school - driving a truck down in Chamberlain. Nothing for him here on the res'."

"Do you have a job, Paxton?" I asked.

"Sure do. I lay flooring of all kinds on the reservation and in surrounding areas. It's a regular forty-hour a week job. Lots of men in the tribe don't work. They hunt and fish and draw a monthly check from the tribe. I would love to hunt and fish all the time, but I like paychecks, too. I'm helping a couple of grandchildren go to college."

"I hear the Sioux give their children Indian names along with regular names," I said.

"Yes," said Paxton. "My Sioux name is Takoda which means friend to everyone."

"That seems to fit," said Mike.

"Now that you mention it," said Paxton, "I have friends from all over. They come here to go fishing. I fish with them whenever I can get away. I try to fish with tribal members, too, but not many of them have boats."

Paxton regaled us for about an hour after dinner with tales of national archery championships, bowling victories, and hunting and fishing trophies. As we got up to leave, Paxton said, "The damned forecast is for winds tomorrow. You may not be able to get out in a boat. Ya might be stuck with shore fishing. Ya got any crappy rigs?"

"What are crappy rigs?" Mike asked.

"Ya might need some help. Tomorrow's Saturday and I don't have to go to work. I have a mobile phone." He wrote his phone number on a scrap of paper.

We heard the wind howl before we got out of bed. One look at the churned-up white caps on Sharpe satisfied us that we couldn't go out in a boat. We ate a cold breakfast in our motel room and wondered what to do.

"Guess we'd better call Paxton," I said.

"Yep," said the others, almost in unison.

We picked up Paxton at his small house in town. "We'd better take two cars. Jim, you can ride with me."

Paxton was wearing a light jacket even though it was pretty chilly, especially considering the wind. At the Iron Nation landing, Paxton parked by the lakeshore. His fishing box contained a number of crappy rigs, stiff twisted wires about three feet long. Attached to the wires and shooting out perpendicular from them were three stiff wire leaders with snelled hooks attached. A heavy sinker was attached to one end of each rig, and a line from a reel to the other. We impaled minnows on the hooks and cast the baited crappy rig from shore out into the lake. Paxton didn't have quite enough complete rigs for all of us, but he jury-rigged a couple.

"Cast out as far as you can," said Paxton.

"But the wind is blowing hard against us," I said.

"That's just the point," said Paxton. "The fish will be coming into this shore where the feed has washed in. When your line is out, put the end of the rod into a holder like this." He jabbed a holder, shaped like a long, stiff spiral, into the ground and inserted the rod handle. "Then reel the line tight so there is an arc in the rod tip. When the arc goes slack, reel in the fish."

On my first cast I snagged up on the bottom and had to break off a crappie rig. "Damn," I said. "I lost one of your rigs."

Paxton stared at me for a bit and then made another crappie rig. "If we can't stand to lose tackle, we shouldn't be fishing," he said.

We soon caught walleyed pike, the targeted fish, but we also caught some good-sized catfish. "Throw them all in the bucket, too. Don't know how many will show up for supper tonight," said Paxton.

"Thought the kids had moved out," I said.

"They did, but my daughter sometimes shows up with her two kids, and no telling how many others are coming. Some of 'em have nowhere else to go. We average ten to twelve every night."

When the fish bucket was mostly full, Paxton reached for his cell phone. "I'm out of coffee," was all he said, and he hung up. Twenty-five minutes later a ten-year-old rusty Ford station wagon chugged up to our fishing spot. Paxton's wife delivered him a fresh thermos of coffee.

"The bucket is over by the truck," was all he said. She dutifully picked up the bucket of fish and headed back home.

et al.

"Wait a second," I said. "What's she going to do with the fish?"

"She'll clean 'em. Whatdoya think?"

"We can clean our own fish, Paxton."

"Don't worry about it. I gave her an electric filet knife for Christmas. She just loves it."

We continued to catch fish, and when we had our limits (including Paxton's higher tribal limit), we took Paxton and the second bucket of fish to Paxton's car. He agreed to have supper with us and said his wife would have our walleyes cleaned and bagged when we picked him up.

"We'd like to pay you a guiding fee," said Mike.

"No," he said. "I want to be your friend, not your guide. But it would be okay to pay my wife a little for cleaning the fish. She can use the money for Christmas presents. Jim, you can ride with me back to the motel."

I got into the passenger seat of his rusty Ford Fairlane, sans seat belts. As Paxton sped to Lower Brule, he said. "Jim, I think I saw a herd of mule deer on top of the hill by the water tower."

Suddenly, he swerved right onto a logging trail, not slowing much. He raced along on a route I wouldn't have wanted to drive a four-wheeler. One bump almost bounced my head on the underside of the roof. Paxton had the stability advantage with a tight grip on the steering wheel. He stared at the rapidly oncoming small trees and bushes and barreled ahead. Then a fallen tree blocked the way, and Paxton slid to an emergency stop, backed up going as fast as he had been going forward, and then proceeded forward on another logging trail. As we approached the water tower, we saw the tails of eight mule deer headed for denser woods. "Did you see 'em, Jim?"

"Yeah, Paxton. That was really something." I hoped he couldn't see me shaking.

He dropped me off at the motel. Mike, Russ, and Big Z were already drinking in our room. "Pour me a stout one," I said. "I just had a wild ride."

My companions just laughed about my adventure with Paxton.

WE PICKED HIM UP at 7:00 PM at his house, a similar structure to its neighbors, all on quarter-acre lots. His house was simple and could have used a new coat of white paint, but the lawn was neatly mowed. His wife brought out four limits of walleyes, each neatly packaged in plastic bags. She turned down our invitation to have supper with us at the casino but thanked us for the twenty-dollar bill Mike gave her for cleaning the fish.

We had a great bull session over dinner. Paxton claimed he once killed a deer at one hundred ten yards with an arrow. He said he used an engine block (probably weighing two hundred pounds) as an anchor in the fast current at the Big Bend Dam outlet. His described the many cars he owned and many odd and kinky repairs necessary to keep them running. He once drove stock cars and had many crazy accidents.

"Paxton what do you tell your wife when you go hunting and fishing all the time?"

"Well," said Paxton, "I just tell her you married me for better or for worse, and this is just part of the worse."

After dinner we went to the parking lot. A lady called out, "I locked my keys in the car, Paxton. Can you help me?"

"Sure," he said. He unscrewed her car's antenna and bent the top to a right angle. He managed to get the antenna down through the bottom of the window and down to the door handle, and he proceeded to push down.

"No, no Paxton," cried the lady. "You have to lift up to open the door."

"No problem," said Paxton. And he removed the antenna and put another bend in it to make a complete hook. Down through the window went the antenna, and this time Paxton pulled up the handle to open the door.

"Thanks," said the woman.

"Nothing to it," said Paxton. And he screwed the grotesquely disfigured antenna back on the car.

Ironically, it turned out her keys were actually left in the casino. The lady drove off with a radio antenna redesigned by Paxton.

RUSS, BIG Z, MIKE, AND I went back to Minnesota the next morning, but Lower Brule was still in our heads. We returned many times over the next twenty years with other friends and relatives, always to be met by a cheerful and willing companion, Paxton. We got to know the wait staff and motel personnel on a first-name basis. There was a short, stocky white cook named "Bubba" who would cook our fish to order. Nothing of ours was ever stolen or damaged. It may be that our friendship with Paxton helped prevent problems, but the locals always seemed genuinely welcoming and friendly. I was ashamed I had been bigoted and prejudiced when I first went to Lower Brule, but now felt at home there with my new friends.

MIKE, RUSS, AND I MET Paxton in the casino one Saturday in late April.

"Where should we fish this year?" I asked.

"They're catching them at Big Bend. Do you think your new boat can go upstream ten miles, Mike?"

et al.

"Sure, Paxton. Just hope the wind stays under twenty. Otherwise it will be a rough and wet ride to and from the primitive ramp."

The next day was very hot. Under blue skies the four of us launched from the primitive ramp and sped over small waves to Big Bend, the widest segment of Lake Sharpe at four miles.

Paxton said, "OK, we should fish with jigs and minnows, either drifting or trolling slow, in eight to ten feet of water."

Paxton, Mike, and I started having bites and catching walleyes right away, but Russ had trouble catching fish.

"What's he doing wrong, Paxton?" asked Mike.

"I've been watching him," said Paxton. "A fish bites and Russ waits and then tries to set the hook. By then, the fish is gone. From this day forward, Russ, you will go by the name Slow Jerk."

Slow Jerk got the message and tried to set the hook sooner, and he caught fish just like the rest of us.

"Well, will you look at that?!" said Mike. He pointed to the sonar screen. The foundations of a house and barn were plainly displayed on the bottom of the lake.

"Yep," said Paxton. "There were plenty of farms and houses flooded over when the dam was built. Even the graveyards where our Lower Brule's ancestors were buried."

"Do Brule Tribal Members carry any resentment over that?"

Paxton took a short breath. "Well, there is some, especially from the older members. You must have noticed a few glares and stares in the casino."

"But the tribe got a nice lake for recreation and irrigation, and even electricity from the turbines at the dam," I said. "Isn't that appreciated?"

"There is a radical element," said Paxton. "Consider what our tribe has lost. Some members have it in for all outsiders. Some even have it in for me. I wasn't born here, and I married a white woman. It's a touchy subject. Let's stop talking about it."

Once again, we caught limits of walleyes, cleaned them, and put them on ice. We returned to the motel in the late afternoon.

THAT EVENING WHEN WE went to dinner, Paxton was waiting for us at the restaurant. The casino bar was gone.

"Hey, Paxton, what happened to the bar?" I asked.

"The Tribal Chairman decided that serving liquor in the casino wasn't worth the trouble it caused," said Paxton.

"Won't be much of a loss for you, huh Paxton?" said Mike.

"No, I don't drink anymore. I had a bad drinking spell years back. Almost lost my family. Family is the most important thing to me, way above fishing and hunting, which is saying something. I don't touch a drop anymore."

et al.

"Can the casino survive without the liquor?" I asked.

"Don't care much if it doesn't," said Paxton. "The gambling money from non-tribal members is okay, but I don't like to see our people at the machines."

"Where does your daughter work now?" asked Mike.

"She's a waitress in Chamberlain. Drives 40 miles each way. I have a hell-of-a-time keeping her car running."

"Can you fish with us tomorrow?" I asked.

"Sure, it's Sunday. Can the guy who I lay floors with come?"

"Any friend of yours is a friend of mine," said Mike.

Paxton said, "I noticed something as we docked at the primitive ramp this afternoon. If the wind stays in the south, we might have a really good day."

THE NEXT MORNING MIKE, Slow Jerk, and I met Paxton and his friend Bill, a small, wiry, older white man. Near the dock, a jetty stretched out from the shore to shelter the landing from south winds. The lake was shallow out beyond the jetty to the south and was deep from the landing area out into the middle of the lake to the north. Puffy white clouds in sunny skies floated by on a south wind.

"Do you guys see a mud line?" asked Paxton.

We all did. The south wind moved water over the shallow, muddy bottom, turning it the color of coffee with cream. After the dark flow hit the deeper water, it turned clear. There was a sharp line between the two.

"Food is being carried into the deeper water, and fish will be feeding on the clear side of the mud line. Let's go get 'em," said Paxton.

Once again Paxton was right. We all got our limits in an hour, four for each of the three white guys and six for Paxton. Mike and I went back to Minneapolis with our possession limits.

IN LATE JUNE THE same year, Mike called Paxton on his cell phone. "My dad and I are coming out Friday. Can you fish with us?"

"Sure. I've got a better job now. I drive the Lower Brule garbage truck. I start by 6:00, but I'm done by 2:00. Best job I ever had. Doesn't pay as much but I can hunt and fish every weekday afternoon and all the weekends besides. You may have to go by yourself Friday morning, but I can go with you Friday afternoon and all day Saturday and Sunday."

Mike said, "Paxton, I want to show you a new trick I've learned. It's called Slow Death, you heard of it?"

"Nope. Always ready to learn," said Paxton.

ON FRIDAY MORNING ABOUT 11:30 Mike and I launched from the primitive landing with ten dozen night crawlers and Slow Death hooks. The hook shanks were curved. When a night crawler was threaded on, and the end of the worm pinched off an inch or so beyond the barb, the bait spun when pulled through the water, triggering a strike reaction from fish even when they weren't hungry. Trolling in various hot spots near the landing, we had our limits in an hour.

Mike called Paxton. "Slow Death is working, and the fish are biting. Come on out and bring relatives or friends."

"I can get off. Be there in an hour," said Paxton.

A rusty Chevy panel truck pulled up to the primitive landing an hour later.

Out stepped Paxton, a young Native American man and a small boy. "Jim, Mike, this is my son-in-law, Dave and my grandson, John. Both are tribal members and can keep six. Now show us this *Slow Death* you've been talking about."

Mike outfitted the five of us with Slow Death rigs. John fished in back of the boat, a premium spot, and caught fish after fish. In an hour we limited out. We went to the cleaning table and fileted twenty-six walleyes.

"Slow Death is pretty impressive," said Paxton. "Most of the tribal members are saying the fish aren't biting. Maybe you guys are learning to fish after all."

"Thanks very much for the fishing trip," said John.

"You are welcome," said Mike. "It was great to fish with you."

"You know, you ought to come back in the fall," said Paxton. "You can go fishing in the morning and I'll go pheasant hunting with you in the afternoon."

"Sounds like a plan," said Mike.

On our way home, I said, "Paxton only has two teeth left on the bottom and three on top. Did you notice?"

"Yep," said Mike. "But he can still eat a ribeye steak when he puts his mind to it. The meat is probably tenderized as it goes down."

MIKE AND I COULDN'T get free until the middle of November, but we were lucky enough to hit a warm spell for a trip out to Lower Brule. On the way out Mike called Paxton from his pickup. "You available Friday afternoon?"

"Oh, hell. I promised to take a couple of widows to Mitchell. They go to the Dollar Store to buy Christmas presents."

"Good god, Paxton. That's eighty miles there and eighty miles back. Does that make sense?"

et al.

"There ain't no Dollar Store in Chamberlain. These women go to Mitchell every year. They don't have no other way to get there if I don't take 'em."

"We'll find the fish on Friday and Saturday morning, then go pheasant hunting Saturday afternoon. Can you go then?" asked Mike.

"By then I'll have all the good hunting spots identified. Tribal land has been pretty good hunting this fall. Pick me up at 1:00."

Friday morning Mike and I went to Iron Nation. I could see my breath and frost covered the dock, but the sun warmed things up by mid-morning. We fished at the stumps and had limits by noon. We continued "catch and release" fishing at some new spots we had never tried. At 3:00 we went back to the motel, iced our fish, and played cribbage until supper. After Bubba cooked some of our fish for dinner, we read and watched TV until bedtime.

After eating a quick breakfast the next morning, we returned to good fishing spots at Iron Nation, caught our limits of walleyes by mid-morning, and iced them down in the motel room. We bought one day pheasant stamps at the reservation game office and had time for a burger at the casino before picking up Paxton at his house at 1:00 PM.

"Head west out of town," said Paxton as he climbed in our pickup with his shotgun without saying 'hello.'

"Nice to see you, Paxton," I said.

"Nice to see you and Mike. I located a farm where the corn has just been picked. The farmer is my friend. Go past Iron Nation and turn south on 61. It's only a few miles."

We parked the pickup and walked a fencerow separating a pasture and a cornfield that was harvested the day before. The sky was bright blue. Long dry grass had turned orange and yellow, and it crackled under our feet. After walking about 50 yards, Paxton cried, "Rooster, rooster," as the whirl of wings broke the quiet. Mike shot, the pheasant fell, and Mike tucked it into the game bag in his coat. We saw two dozen more birds, some roosters and some hens. We finished hunting the edge of the cornfield, and only due to my poor shooting, were we still three roosters short of our limits.

Paxton lit a cigarette. "I know a good place on reservation land," he said. "We'll fill out there."

We drove to dry, upland fields comprising twenty full sections of corn and milo. Some fields had trees planted at the fence lines, and we stopped at one of those. Paxton said, "We'll hunt here. I'll drive your pickup to the end of the fence line and block for you. Jim and Mike, you should walk along opposite sides of the fence. You may flush a few on the way, and as you get close to me, those birds running ahead will fly."

When Paxton left, I asked Mike, "Did you notice Paxton was short of breath at the last spot."

"Yes. And his color isn't good either. He could be having health issues. I wish he didn't chain-smoke."

Mike and I walked the mile to Paxton and shot two roosters as we got close to the pickup. Then Paxton drove the pickup another mile and blocked at the end of another section line. As we approached Paxton, we flushed a rooster. Paxton didn't miss.

"That fills us out," said Mike. "Let's eat lunch out here and then go back to the motel and clean the birds."

"What ya got for lunch?" asked Paxton.

"Ham and cheese sandwiches and apples." replied Mike.

"I can eat a sandwich, but can't eat apples anymore," said Paxton.

I thought about how hard it would be to eat an apple with just a few teeth. "How about if I peel an apple for you?" I asked.

"Sure, if it wouldn't be too much trouble."

I took my utility pocketknife from its holster, cut the skin off the apple, quartered and cored it, and handed the pieces to Paxton. He ate them eagerly. "Thanks. I can't remember the last time I had an apple," he said.

"No problem", I replied.

Back at the motel, a large dumpster served as a receptacle for pheasant feathers and guts, and I carried five-gallon pails of water filled from a spigot on the outside wall of the motel. Three of us working diligently were able to complete the cleaning task in about an hour.

"Paxton," said Mike, "Dad and I need only two birds apiece. Could you use the rest?"

"Sure," said Paxton, "Our freezer is getting a little low. My wife really appreciates all the birds she can get. By the way, the next time you guys see me, I'll be wearing false teeth. The ones I have left always get infected. It will be a relief."

Mike and I were content to drive home with our pheasants and walleyes, and to spend the winter recalling our wonderful fishing and hunting experiences with Paxton.

THE NEXT SPRING MIKE called Paxton from Minnesota in April. "How's fishing, Paxton?"

"Don't rightly know, I haven't been out. Had me a little problem with a heart attack and have been laid up all winter and spring."

"Gee, sorry to hear it."

"The doctor in Pierre put in a stint. Said I should be up and around by fall."

"Can't you at least have supper with us when we come out?" asked Mike.

"Don't think so. I'm supposed to stay in bed."

et al.

"Look forward to seeing you in the fall," said Mike.

"It's a deal," said Paxton.

We fished without Paxton and caught limits of fish. But it just wasn't the same.

IN OCTOBER MIKE AND I called Paxton using a speakerphone. "We're coming up. Want to fish Friday?"

"Sure. I can fish any time I want. They retired me after that heart attack. I can fish this Friday, but not Saturday. That's the opening of the tribal deer season. I really wanted to go bow hunting, but I don't have the strength to pull my 75-pound bow. But I do have a muzzle loader buck tag."

"Meet us at Iron Nation Friday at noon."

"See you there." Mike hung up.

I asked, "Mike, what's a muzzle loader?"

"It's a really old-style rifle similar to the ones colonial soldiers used, but with some improvements. You tamp in gun power pellets in the barrel, and then a 50-caliber riffled slug, and finally mount an igniter by the hammer. After a shot it takes at least a minute to reload. You only get one shot with a muzzle loader."

Friday at noon we pulled up to the dock at Iron Nation and Paxton got on. He looked healthier but had lost weight. His teeth had been pulled, but he didn't have false teeth.

"Good to see you Paxton," I said.

"Jim and Mike, it's good to see you, too."

"Where's fishing been good lately?"

"Heard Joe Creek has been good."

"Then that's where we're headed," said Mike.

Fishing was very good eight miles upstream from Iron Nation at Joe Creek, and we filled out in two hours. "Let's have lunch before we go back," said Mike.

We rode back to Iron Nation, and while Mike and I cleaned the fish, Paxton carried water and helped rinse the filets. Surprisingly, Paxton was no good at cleaning fish. He was out of practice by forty years because his wife always performed that task.

"By the way, my granddaughter is getting a degree this spring, the first person in my family to get one. I'm really proud of her. She's practice-teaching in Pierre this term."

"Congratulations, Paxton," I said.

"What happened to the false teeth," I asked.

et al.

"Medicare paid for pulling the teeth, but wouldn't cover the choppers. Ran out of money or something. Couldn't cover the $1600 myself. But I'll get by."

"That's the government for you," said Slow Jerk.

THE NEXT DAY MIKE and I drove to Iron Nation, and on our way, we saw a big mule deer and a doe not far from the road. Mike got on the phone to Paxton. "We saw a buck you might like on our way to fish. He and a doe were north of the road about a half mile from Iron Nation."

"Thanks, Mike. I'm on my way."

We launched in the bay, and as we landed our third fish, we heard a shot. "That's Paxton," said Mike.

We kept fishing for a while, and then Mike's cell phone rang. "I think I got him," said Paxton. "I could use some help in finding him and loading him into my van."

"Sure enough," said Mike. "Meet you right away in the Iron Nation parking lot."

Five minutes later Paxton came. He was still excited; his hand even shook a little. "Climb in. I know a back road."

He drove off through a pasture into woods and kept going. The van heaved and rolled over rough terrain. Then he stopped to get his bearings. "See that fence post down there along the road.

That's the one I used to steady my gun. I shot from there up to here, and the buck should be around."

The post was far away. It looked like a half a matchstick.

We spread out, searching. "I found him," cried Paxton. The deer was lying in a pool of blood, quite dead.

I looked back at the fencepost. "That shot was most of 200 yards," I said.. We later measured it at 172 years with a range finder.

"With open sights, too. That was amazing," said Mike.

"Congratulations, Paxton," I said.

He smiled, looking very pleased. He called his wife and said, "I shot a good-sized buck. Our freezer will be full again."

Paxton field-dressed the deer, and we loaded it into his vehicle. Paxton dropped us off back at Iron Nation, and we continued fishing while he took the deer to a processing shop.

"I think we should buy Paxton his false teeth," I said.

"I'll chip in," said Mike.

"Me, too," declared Slow Jerk. "Look at all that man has done for us."

"Then I'll send him a cashier's check when we get back to Minneapolis. You two can contribute when we settle up at the motel.

et al.

After the check was sent and cashed, we waited a month. Mike got a call.

"I'm incredibly grateful to you guys. I thought I might just take a bite out of an apple and send that to Jim. Instead here is a picture of me wearing my new teeth. Don't I look handsome?"

"No problem, Paxton. Looking forward to fishing with you in the spring."

"Me, too," he said.

I KNOW PAXTON WON'T always be with us. In the little, poorly tended cemetery north of Lower Brule, a simple white cross will mark his remains, but I'm not ready to write his obituary yet. I hope to have more good times with this amazing man at my home away from home in Lower Brule. He spent his life concentrating on the only things that really mattered to him; his family and fishing and hunting. He has lived a life between two cultures, that of his tribe and that of white people, and succeeded in being a friend to all.

51336045R00150

Made in the USA
Columbia, SC
20 February 2019